B.C Brown

Ormond
Volume 3

outlook

B.C Brown

Ormond
Volume 3

1st Edition | ISBN: 978-3-75238-259-4

Place of Publication: Frankfurt am Main, Germany

Year of Publication: 2020

Outlook Verlag GmbH, Germany.

Reproduction of the original.

ORMOND

B.C. BROWN

VOL. III.

CHAPTER I.

"My father, in proportion as he grew old and rich, became weary of Aleppo. His natal soil, had it been the haunt of Calmucks or Bedouins, his fancy would have transformed into Paradise. No wonder that the equitable aristocracy and the peaceful husbandmen of Ragusa should be endeared to his heart by comparison with Egyptian plagues and Turkish tyranny. Besides, he lived for his children as well as himself. Their education and future lot required him to seek a permanent home.

"He embarked, with his wife and offspring, at Scanderoon. No immediate conveyance to Ragusa offering, the appearance of the plague in Syria induced him to hasten his departure. He entered a French vessel for Marseilles. After being three days at sea, one of the crew was seized by the fatal disease which had depopulated all the towns upon the coast. The voyage was made with more than usual despatch; but, before we reached our port, my mother and half the crew perished. My father died in the Lazaretto, more through grief than disease.

"My brother and I were children and helpless. My father's fortune was on board this vessel, and was left by his death to the mercy of the captain. This man was honest, and consigned us and our property to the merchant with whom he dealt. Happily for us, our protector was childless and of scrupulous integrity. We henceforth became his adopted children. My brother's education and my own were conducted on the justest principles.

"At the end of four years, our protector found it expedient to make a voyage to Cayenne. His brother was an extensive proprietor in that colony, but his sudden death made way for the succession of our friend. To establish his claims, his presence was necessary on the spot. He was little qualified for arduous enterprises, and his age demanded repose; but, his own acquisitions having been small, and being desirous of leaving us in possession of competence, he cheerfully embarked.

"Meanwhile, my brother was placed at a celebrated seminary in the Pays de Vaud, and I was sent to a sister who resided at Verona. I was at this time fourteen years old,—one year younger than my brother, whom, since that period, I have neither heard of nor seen.

"I was now a woman, and qualified to judge and act for myself. The character of my new friend was austere and devout, and there were so many incongenial points between us that but little tranquillity was enjoyed under her control. The priest who discharged the office of her confessor thought proper to entertain views with regard to me, grossly inconsistent with the sanctity of his profession. He was a man of profound dissimulation and masterly address. His efforts, however, were repelled with disdain. My security against his attempts lay in the uncouthness and deformity which nature had bestowed upon his person and visage, rather than in the firmness of my own principles.

"The courtship of Father Bartoli, the austerities of Madame Roselli, the disgustful or insipid occupations to which I was condemned, made me impatiently wish for a change; but my father (so I will call him) had decreed that I should remain under his sister's guardianship till his return from Guiana. When this would happen was uncertain. Events unforeseen might protract it for years, but it could not arrive in less than a twelvemonth.

"I was incessantly preyed upon by discontent. My solitude was loathsome. I panted after liberty and friendship, and the want of these were not recompensed by luxury and quiet, and by the instructions in useful science which I received from Bartoli, who, though detested as a hypocrite and lover, was venerable as a scholar. He would fain have been an Abelard, but it was not his fate to meet with an Eloisa.

"Two years passed away in this durance. My miseries were exquisite. I am almost at a loss to account for the unhappiness of that time, for, looking back upon it, I perceive that an equal period could not have been spent with more benefit. For the sake of being near me, Bartoli importunately offered his instructions. He had nothing to communicate but metaphysics and geometry. These were little to my taste, but I could not keep him at a distance. I had no other alternative than to endure him as a lover or a teacher. His passion for science was at least equal to that which ho entertained for me, and both these passions combined to make him a sedulous instructor. He was a disciple of the newest doctrines respecting matter and mind. He denied the impenetrability of the first, and the immateriality of the second. These he endeavoured to inculcate upon me, as well as to subvert my religious tenets, because he delighted, like all men, in transfusing his opinions, and because he regarded my piety as the only obstacle to his designs. He succeeded in dissolving the spell of ignorance, but not in producing that kind of acquiescence he wished. He had, in this respect, to struggle not only with my principles, but my weakness. He might have overcome every obstacle but my

3

abhorrence of deformity and age. To cure me of this aversion was beyond his power. My servitude grew daily more painful. I grew tired of chasing a comet to its aphelion, and of untying the knot of an infinite series. A change in my condition became indispensable to my very existence. Languor and sadness, and unwillingness to eat or to move, were at last my perpetual attendants!

"Madame Roselli was alarmed at my condition. The sources of my inquietude were incomprehensible to her. The truth was, that I scarcely understood them myself, and my endeavours to explain them to my friend merely instilled into her an opinion that I was either lunatic or deceitful. She complained and admonished; but my disinclination to my usual employments would not be conquered, and my health rapidly declined. A physician, who was called, confessed that my case was beyond his power to understand, but recommended, as a sort of desperate expedient, a change of scene. A succession and variety of objects might possibly contribute to my cure.

"At this time there arrived, at Verona, Lady D'Arcy,—an Englishwoman of fortune and rank, and a strenuous Catholic. Her husband had lately died; and, in order to divert her grief, as well as to gratify her curiosity in viewing the great seat of her religion, she had come to Italy. Intercourse took place between her and Madame Roselli. By this means she gained a knowledge of my person and condition, and kindly offered to take me under her protection. She meant to traverse every part of Italy, and was willing that I should accompany her in all her wanderings.

"This offer was gratefully accepted, in spite of the artifices and remonstrances of Bartoli. My companion speedily contracted for me the affection of a mother. She was without kindred of her own religion, having acquired her faith, not by inheritance, but conversion. She desired to abjure her native country, and to bind herself, by every social tie, to a people who adhered to the same faith. Me she promised to adopt as her daughter, provided her first impressions in my favour were not belied by my future deportment.

"My principles were opposite to hers; but habit, an aversion to displease my friend, my passion for knowledge, which my new condition enabled me to gratify, all combined to make me a deceiver. But my imposture was merely of a negative kind; I deceived her rather by forbearance to contradict, and by acting as she acted, than by open assent and zealous concurrence. My new state was, on this account, not devoid of inconvenience. The general deportment and sentiments of Lady D'Arcy testified a vigorous and pure mind. New avenues to knowledge, by converse with mankind and with books, and by the survey of new scenes, were open for my use. Gratitude and veneration attached me to my friend, and made the task of pleasing her, by a seeming conformity of sentiments, less irksome.

4

"During this interval, no tidings were received by his sister, at Verona, respecting the fate of Sebastian Roselli. The supposition of his death was too plausible not to be adopted. What influence this disaster possessed over my brother's destiny, I know not. The generosity of Lady D'Arcy hindered me from experiencing any disadvantage from this circumstance. Fortune seemed to have decreed that I should not be reduced to the condition of an orphan.

"At an age and in a situation like mine, I could not remain long unacquainted with love. My abode at Rome introduced me to the knowledge of a youth from England, who had every property which I regarded as worthy of esteem. He was a kinsman of—Lady D'Arcy, and as such admitted at her house on the most familiar footing. His patrimony was extremely slender, but was in his own possession. He had no intention of increasing it by any professional pursuit, but was contented with the frugal provision it afforded. He proposed no other end of his existence than the acquisition of virtue and knowledge.

"The property of Lady D'Arcy was subject to her own disposal, but, on the failure of a testament, this youth was, in legal succession, the next heir. He was well acquainted with her temper and views, but, in the midst of urbanity and gentleness, studied none of those concealments of opinion which would have secured him her favour. That he was not of her own faith was an insuperable, but the only, obstacle to the admission of his claims.

"If conformity of age and opinions, and the mutual fascination of love, be a suitable basis for marriage, Wentworth and I were destined for each other. Mutual disclosure added sanctity to our affection; but, the happiness of Lady D'Arcy being made to depend upon the dissolution of our compact, the heroism of Wentworth made him hasten to dissolve it. As soon as she discovered our attachment, she displayed symptoms of the deepest anguish. In addition to religious motives, her fondness for me forbade her to exist but in my society and in the belief of the purity of my faith. The contention, on my part, was vehement between the regards due to her felicity and to my own. Had Wentworth left me the power to decide, my decision would doubtless have evinced the frailty of my fortitude and the strength of my passion; but, having informed me fully of the reasons of his conduct, he precipitately retired from Rome. He left me no means of tracing his footsteps and of assailing his weakness by expostulation and entreaty.

"Lady D'Arcy was no less eager to abandon a spot where her happiness had been so imminently endangered. Our next residence was Palermo. I will not dwell upon the sensations produced by this disappointment in me. I review them with astonishment and self-compassion. If I thought it possible for me to sink again into imbecility so ignominious, I should be disposed to kill myself.

"There was no end to vows of fondness and tokens of gratitude in Lady

D'Arcy. Her future life should be devoted to compensate me for this sacrifice. Nothing could console her in that single state in which she intended to live, but the consolations of my fellowship. Her conduct coincided for some time with these professions, and my anguish was allayed by the contemplation of the happiness conferred upon one whom I revered.

"My friend could not be charged with dissimulation and artifice. Her character had been mistaken by herself as well as by me. Devout affections seemed to have filled her heart, to the exclusion of any object besides myself. She cherished with romantic tenderness the memory of her husband, and imagined that a single state was indispensably enjoined upon her by religious duty. This persuasion, however, was subverted by the arts of a Spanish cavalier, young, opulent, and romantic as herself in devotion. An event like this might, indeed, have been easily predicted, by those who reflected that the lady was still in the bloom of life, ardent in her temper, and bewitching in her manners.

"The fondness she had lavished upon me was now, in some degree, transferred to a new object; but I still received the treatment due to a beloved daughter. She was solicitous as ever to promote my gratification, and a diminution of kindness would not have been suspected by those who had not witnessed the excesses of her former passion. Her marriage with the Spaniard removed the obstacle to union with Wentworth. This man, however, had set himself beyond the reach of my inquiries. Had there been the shadow of a clue afforded me, I should certainly have sought him to the ends of the world.

"I continued to reside with my friend, and accompanied her and her husband to Spain. Antonio de Leyva was a man of probity. His mind was enlightened by knowledge and his actions dictated by humanity. Though but little older than myself, and young enough to be the son of his spouse, his deportment to me was a model of rectitude and delicacy. I spent a year in Spain, partly in the mountains of Castile and partly at Segovia. New manners and a new language occupied my attention for a time; but these, losing their novelty, lost their power to please. I betook myself to books, to beguile the tediousness and diversify the tenor of my life.

"This would not have long availed; but I was relieved from new repinings, by the appointment of Antonio de Leyva to a diplomatic office at Vienna. Thither we accordingly repaired. A coincidence of circumstances had led me wide from the path of ambition and study usually allotted to my sex and age. From the computation of eclipses, I now betook myself to the study of man. My proficiency, when I allowed it to be seen, attracted great attention. Instead of adulation and gallantry, I was engaged in watching the conduct of states and revolving the theories of politicians.

"Superficial observers were either incredulous with regard to my character, or connected a stupid wonder with their belief. My attainments and habits they did not see to be perfectly consonant with the principles of human nature. They unavoidably flowed from the illicit attachment of Bartoli, and the erring magnanimity of Wentworth. Aversion to the priest was the grand inciter of my former studies; the love of Wentworth, whom I hoped once more to meet, made me labour to exclude the importunities of others, and to qualify myself for securing his affections.

"Since our parting in Italy, Wentworth had traversed Syria and Egypt, and arrived some months after me at Vienna. He was on the point of leaving the city, when accident informed me of his being there. An interview was effected, and, our former sentiments respecting each other having undergone no change, we were united. Madame de Leyva reluctantly concurred with our wishes, and, at parting, forced upon me a considerable sum of money.

"Wentworth's was a character not frequently met with in the world. He was a political enthusiast, who esteemed nothing more graceful or glorious than to die for the liberties of mankind. He had traversed Greece with an imagination full of the exploits of ancient times, and derived, from contemplating Thermopylæ and Marathon, an enthusiasm that bordered upon frenzy.

"It was now the third year of the Revolutionary War in America, and, previous to our meeting at Vienna, he had formed the resolution of repairing thither and tendering his service to the Congress as a volunteer. Our marriage made no change in his plans. My soul was engrossed by two passions,—a wild spirit of adventure, and a boundless devotion to him. I vowed to accompany him in every danger, to vie with him in military ardour, to combat and to die by his side.

"I delighted to assume the male dress, to acquire skill at the sword, and dexterity in every boisterous exercise. The timidity that commonly attends women gradually vanished. I felt as if imbued by a soul that was a stranger to the sexual distinction. We embarked at Brest, in a frigate destined for St. Domingo. A desperate conflict with an English ship in the Bay of Biscay was my first introduction to a scene of tumult and danger of whose true nature I had formed no previous conception. At first I was spiritless and full of dismay. Experience, however, gradually reconciled me to the life that I had chosen.

"A fortunate shot, by dismasting the enemy, allowed us to prosecute our voyage unmolested. At Cape François we found a ship which transported us, after various perils, to Richmond, in Virginia. I will not carry you through the adventures of four years. You, sitting all your life in peaceful corners, can scarcely imagine that variety of hardship and turmoil which attends the

7

female who lives in a camp.

"Few would sustain these hardships with better grace than I did. I could seldom be prevailed on to remain at a distance, and inactive, when my husband was in battle, and more than once rescued him from death by the seasonable destruction of his adversary.

"At the repulse of the Americans at Germantown, Wentworth was wounded and taken prisoner. I obtained permission to attend his sick-bed and supply that care without which he would assuredly have died. Being imperfectly recovered, he was sent to England and subjected to a rigorous imprisonment. Milder treatment might have permitted his complete restoration to health; but, as it was, he died.

"His kindred were noble, and rich, and powerful; but it was difficult to make them acquainted with Wentworth's situation. Their assistance, when demanded, was readily afforded; but it came too late to prevent his death. Me they snatched from my voluntary prison, and employed every friendly art to efface from my mind the images of recent calamity.

"Wentworth's singularities of conduct and opinion had estranged him at an early age from his family. They felt little regret at his fate, but every motive concurred to secure their affection and succour to me. My character was known to many officers, returned from America, whose report, joined with the influence of my conversation, rendered me an object to be gazed at by thousands. Strange vicissitude! Now immersed in the infection of a military hospital, the sport of a wayward fortune, struggling with cold and hunger, with negligence and contumely. A month after, passing into scenes of gayety and luxury, exhibited at operas and masquerades, made the theme of inquiry and encomium at every place of resort, and caressed by the most illustrious among the votaries of science and the advocates of the American cause.

"Here I again met Madame de Leyva. This woman was perpetually assuming new forms. She was a sincere convert to the Catholic religion, but she was open to every new impression. She was the dupe of every powerful reasoner, and assumed with equal facility the most opposite shapes. She had again reverted to the Protestant religion, and, governed by a headlong zeal in whatever cause she engaged, she had sacrificed her husband and child to a new conviction.

"The instrument of this change was a man who passed, at that time, for a Frenchman. He was young, accomplished, and addressful, but was not suspected of having been prompted by illicit views, or of having seduced the lady from allegiance to her husband as well as to her God. De Leyva, however, who was sincere in his religion as well as his love, was hasty to avenge this injury, and, in a contest with the Frenchman, was killed. His wife adopted at once her ancient religion and country, and was once more an Englishwoman.

"At our meeting her affection for me seemed to be revived, and the most passionate entreaties were used to detain me in England. My previous arrangements would not suffer it. I foresaw restraints and inconveniences from the violence and caprice of her passions, and intended henceforth to keep my liberty inviolate by any species of engagement, either of friendship or marriage. My habits were French, and I proposed henceforward to take up my abode at Paris. Since his voyage to Guiana, I had heard no tidings of Sebastian Roselli. This man's image was cherished with filial emotions, and I conceived that the sight of him would amply reward a longer journey than from London to Marseilles.

"Beyond my hopes, I found him in his ancient abode. The voyage, and a residence of three years at Cayenne, had been beneficial to his appearance and health. He greeted me with paternal tenderness, and admitted me to a full participation of his fortune, which the sale of his American property had greatly enhanced. He was a stranger to the fate of my brother. On his return home he had gone to Switzerland, with a view of ascertaining his destiny. The youth, a few months after his arrival at Lausanne, had eloped with a companion, and had hitherto eluded all Roselli's searches and inquiries. My father was easily prevailed upon to transfer his residence from Provence to Paris."

Here Martinette paused, and, marking the clock, "It is time," resumed she, "to begone. Are you not weary of my tale? On the day I entered France, I entered the twenty-third year of my age, so that my promise of detailing my youthful adventures is fulfilled. I must away. Till we meet again, farewell."

CHAPTER II.

Such was the wild series of Martinette's adventures. Each incident fastened on the memory of Constantia, and gave birth to numberless reflections. Her prospect of mankind seemed to be enlarged, on a sudden, to double its ancient dimensions. Ormond's narratives had carried her beyond the Mississippi, and into the deserts of Siberia. He had recounted the perils of a Russian war, and painted the manners of Mongols and Naudowessies. Her new friend had led her back to the civilized world and portrayed the other half of the species. Men, in their two forms of savage and refined, had been scrutinized by these observers; and what was wanting in the delineations of the one was liberally supplied by the other.

Eleven years in the life of Martinette was unrelated. Her conversation suggested the opinion that this interval had been spent in France. It was obvious to suppose that a woman thus fearless and sagacious had not been inactive at a period like the present, which called forth talents and courage without distinction of sex, and had been particularly distinguished by female enterprise and heroism. Her name easily led to the suspicion of concurrence with the subverters of monarchy, and of participation in their fall. Her flight from the merciless tribunals of the faction that now reigned would explain present appearances.

Martinette brought to their next interview an air of uncommon exultation. On this being remarked, she communicated the tidings of the fall of the sanguinary tyranny of Robespierre. Her eyes sparkled, and every feature was pregnant with delight, while she unfolded, with her accustomed energy, the particulars of this tremendous revolution. The blood which it occasioned to flow was mentioned without any symptoms of disgust or horror.

Constantia ventured to ask if this incident was likely to influence her own condition.

"Yes. It will open the way for my return."

"Then you think of returning to a scene of so much danger?"

"Danger, my girl? It is my element. I am an adorer of liberty, and liberty without peril can never exist."

"But so much bloodshed and injustice! Does not your heart shrink from the view of a scene of massacre and tumult, such as Paris has lately exhibited and will probably continue to exhibit?"

"Thou talkest, Constantia, in a way scarcely worthy of thy good sense. Have I not been three years in a camp? What are bleeding wounds and mangled corpses, when accustomed to the daily sight of them for years? Am I not a lover of liberty? and must I not exult in the fall of tyrants, and regret only that my hand had no share in their destruction?"

"But a woman—how can the heart of woman be inured to the shedding of blood?"

"Have women, I beseech thee, no capacity to reason and infer? Are they less open than men to the influence of habit? My hand never faltered when liberty demanded the victim. If thou wert with me at Paris, I could show thee a fusil of two barrels, which is precious beyond any other relic, merely because it enabled me to kill thirteen officers at Jemappe. Two of these were emigrant nobles, whom I knew and loved before the Revolution, but the cause they had since espoused cancelled their claims to mercy."

"What!" said the startled Constantia; "have you fought in the ranks?"

"Certainly. Hundreds of my sex have done the same. Some were impelled by the enthusiasm of love, and some by a mere passion for war; some by the contagion of example; and some—with whom I myself must be ranked—by a generous devotion to liberty. Brunswick and Saxe-Coburg had to contend with whole regiments of women,—regiments they would have formed, if they had been collected into separate bodies.

"I will tell thee a secret. Thou wouldst never have seen Martinette de Beauvais, if Brunswick had deferred one day longer his orders for retreating into Germany."

"How so?"

"She would have died by her own hand."

"What could lead to such an outrage?"

"The love of liberty."

"I cannot comprehend how that love should prompt you to suicide."

"I will tell thee. The plan was formed, and could not miscarry. A woman was to play the part of a banished Royalist, was to repair to the Prussian camp, and to gain admission to the general. This would have easily been granted to a female and an ex-noble. There she was to assassinate the enemy of her country, and to attest her magnanimity by slaughtering herself. I was weak enough to regret the ignominious retreat of the Prussians, because it precluded the necessity of such a sacrifice."

This was related with accents and looks that sufficiently attested its truth. Constantia shuddered, and drew back, to contemplate more deliberately the features of her guest. Hitherto she had read in them nothing that bespoke the desperate courage of a martyr and the deep designing of an assassin. The image which her mind had reflected from the deportment of this woman was changed. The likeness which she had, feigned to herself was no longer seen. She felt that antipathy was preparing to displace love. These sentiments, however, she concealed, and suffered the conversation to proceed.

Their discourse now turned upon the exploits of several women who mingled in the tumults of the capital and in the armies on the frontiers. Instances were mentioned of ferocity in some, and magnanimity in others, which almost surpassed belief. Constantia listened greedily, though not with approbation,

11

and acquired, at every sentence, new desire to be acquainted with the personal history of Martinette. On mentioning this wish, her friend said that she endeavoured to amuse her exile by composing her own memoirs, and that, on her next visit, she would bring with her the volume, which she would suffer Constantia to read.

A separation of a week elapsed. She felt some impatience for the renewal of their intercourse, and for the perusal of the volume that had been mentioned. One evening Sarah Baxter, whom Constantia had placed in her own occasional service, entered the room with marks of great joy and surprise, and informed her that she at length had discovered Miss Monrose. From her abrupt and prolix account, it appeared that Sarah had overtaken Miss Monrose in the street, and, guided by her own curiosity, as well as by the wish to gratify her mistress, she had followed the stranger. To her utter astonishment, the lady had paused at Mr. Dudley's door, with a seeming resolution to enter it, but presently resumed her way. Instead of pursuing her steps farther, Sarah had stopped to communicate this intelligence to Constantia. Having delivered her news, she hastened away, but, returning, in a moment, with a countenance of new surprise, she informed her mistress that on leaving the house she had met Miss Monrose at the door, on the point of entering. She added that the stranger had inquired for Constantia, and was now waiting below.

Constantia took no time to reflect upon an incident so unexpected and so strange, but proceeded forthwith to the parlour. Martinette only was there. It did not instantly occur to her that this lady and Mademoiselle Monrose might possibly be the same. The inquiries she made speedily removed her doubts, and it now appeared that the woman about whose destiny she had formed so many conjectures and fostered so much anxiety was no other than the daughter of Roselli.

Having readily answered her questions, Martinette inquired, in her turn, into the motives of her friend's curiosity. These were explained by a succinct account of the transactions to which the deceased Baxter had been a witness. Constantia concluded with mentioning her own reflections on the tale, and intimating her wish to be informed how Martinette had extricated herself from a situation so calamitous.

"Is there any room for wonder on that head?" replied the guest. "It was absurd to stay longer in the house. Having finished the interment of Roselli, (soldier-fashion,) for he was the man who suffered his foolish regrets to destroy him, I forsook the house. Roselli was by no means poor, but he could not consent to live at ease, or to live at all, while his country endured such horrible oppressions, and when so many of his friends had perished. I complied with his humour, because it could not be changed, and I revered him too much to desert him."

"But whither," said Constantia, "could you seek shelter at a time like that? The city was desolate, and a wandering female could scarcely be received under any roof. All inhabited houses were closed at that hour, and the fear of infection would have shut them against you if they had not been already so."

"Hast thou forgotten that there were at that time at least ten thousand French in this city, fugitives from Marat and from St. Domingo? That they lived in utter fearlessness of the reigning disease,—sung and loitered in the public walks, and prattled at their doors, with all their customary unconcern? Supposest thou that there were none among these who would receive a countrywoman, even if her name had not been Martinette de Beauvais? Thy fancy has depicted strange things; but believe me that, without a farthing and without a name, I should not have incurred the slightest inconvenience. The death of Roselli I foresaw, because it was gradual in its approach, and was sought by him as a good. My grief, therefore, was exhausted before it came, and I rejoiced at his death, because it was the close of all his sorrows. The rueful pictures of my distress and weakness which were given by Baxter existed only in his own fancy."

Martinette pleaded an engagement, and took her leave, professing to have come merely to leave with her the promised manuscript. This interview, though short, was productive of many reflections on the deceitfulness of appearances, and on the variety of maxims by which the conduct of human beings is regulated. She was accustomed to impart all her thoughts and relate every new incident to her father. With this view she now hied to his apartment. This hour it was her custom, when disengaged, always to spend with him.

She found Mr. Dudley busy in revolving a scheme which various circumstances had suggested and gradually conducted to maturity. No period of his life had been equally delightful with that portion of his youth which he had spent in Italy. The climate, the language, the manners of the people, and the sources of intellectual gratification in painting and music, were congenial to his taste. He had reluctantly forsaken these enchanting seats, at the summons of his father, but, on his return to his native country, had encountered nothing but ignominy and pain. Poverty and blindness had beset his path, and it seemed as if it were impossible to fly too far from the scene of his disasters. His misfortunes could not be concealed from others, and every thing around him seemed to renew the memory of all that he had suffered. All the events of his youth served to entice him to Italy, while all the incidents of his subsequent life concurred to render disgustful his present abode.

His daughter's happiness was not to be forgotten. This he imagined would be eminently promoted by the scheme. It would open to her new avenues to knowledge. It would snatch her from the odious pursuit of Ormond, and, by a variety of objects and adventures, efface from her mind any impression which his dangerous artifices might have made upon it.

This project was now communicated to Constantia. Every argument adapted to influence her choice was employed. He justly conceived that the only obstacle to her adoption of it related to Ormond. He expatiated on the dubious character of this man, the wildness of his schemes, and the magnitude of his errors. What could be expected from a man, half of whose life had been spent at the head of a band of Cossacks, spreading devastation in the regions of the Danube, and supporting by flagitious intrigues the tyranny of Catharine, and the other half in traversing inhospitable countries, and extinguishing what remained of clemency and justice by intercourse with savages?

It was admitted that his energies were great, but misdirected, and that to restore them to the guidance of truth was not in itself impossible; but it was so with relation to any power that she possessed. Conformity would flow from their marriage, but this conformity was not to be expected from him. It was not his custom to abjure any of his doctrines or recede from any of his claims. She knew likewise the conditions of their union. She must go with him to some corner of the world where his boasted system was established. What was the road to it he had carefully concealed, but it was evident that it lay beyond the precincts of civilized existence.

Whatever were her ultimate decision, it was at least proper to delay it. Six years were yet wanting of that period at which only she formerly considered marriage as proper. To all the general motives for deferring her choice, the conduct of Ormond superadded the weightiest. Their correspondence might continue, but her residence in Europe and converse with mankind might enlighten her judgement and qualify her for a more rational decision.

Constantia was not uninfluenced by these reasonings. Instead of reluctantly admitting them, she somewhat wondered that they had not been suggested by her own reflections. Her imagination anticipated her entrance on that mighty scene with emotions little less than rapturous. Her studies had conferred a thousand ideal charms on a theatre where Scipio and Cæsar had performed their parts. Her wishes were no less importunate to gaze upon the Alps and Pyrenees, and to vivify and chasten the images collected from books, by comparing them with their real prototypes.

No social ties existed to hold her to America. Her only kinsman and friend would be the companion of her journeys. This project was likewise recommended by advantages of which she only was qualified to judge. Sophia Westwyn had embarked, four years previous to this date, for England, in company with an English lady and her husband. The arrangements that were made forbade either of the friends to hope for a future meeting. Yet now, by virtue of this project, this meeting seemed no longer to be hopeless.

This burst of new ideas and now hopes on the mind of Constantia took place in the course of a single hour. No change in her external situation had been wrought, and yet her mind had undergone the most signal revolution. Tho novelty as well as greatness of the prospect kept her in a state of elevation and awe, more ravishing than any she had ever experienced. Anticipations of intercourse with nature in her most august forms, with men in diversified states of society, with the posterity of Greeks and Romans, and with the actors that were now upon the stage, and, above all, with the being whom absence and the want of other attachments had, in some sort, contributed to deify, made this night pass away upon the wings of transport.

The hesitation which existed on parting with her father speedily gave place to an ardour impatient of the least delay. She saw no impediments to the immediate commencement of the voyage. To delay it a month, or even a week, seemed to be unprofitable tardiness. In this ferment of her thoughts, she was neither able nor willing to sleep. In arranging the means of departure and anticipating the events that would successively arise, there was abundant food for contemplation.

She marked the first dawnings of the day, and rose. She felt reluctance to break upon her father's morning slumbers, but considered that her motives were extremely urgent, and that the pleasure afforded him by her zealous approbation of his scheme would amply compensate him for this unseasonable intrusion on his rest. She hastened therefore to his chamber. She entered with blithesome steps, and softly drew aside the curtain.

CHAPTER III.

Unhappy Constantia! At the moment when thy dearest hopes had budded afresh, when the clouds of insecurity and disquiet had retired from thy vision, wast thou assailed by the great subverter of human schemes. Thou sawest nothing in futurity but an eternal variation and succession of delights. Thou wast hastening to forget dangers and sorrows which thou fondly imaginedst were never to return. This day was to be the outset of a new career; existence was henceforth to be embellished with enjoyments hitherto scarcely within the reach of hope.

Alas! thy predictions of calamity seldom failed to be verified. Not so thy prognostics of pleasure. These, though fortified by every calculation of contingencies, were edifices grounded upon nothing. Thy life was a struggle with malignant destiny,—a contest for happiness in which thou wast fated to be overcome.

She stooped to kiss the venerable cheek of her father, and, by whispering, to break his slumber. Her eye was no sooner fixed upon his countenance, than she started back and shrieked. She had no power to forbear. Her outcries were piercing and vehement. They ceased only with the cessation of breath. She sunk upon a chair in a state partaking more of death than of life, mechanically prompted to give vent to her agonies in shrieks, but incapable of uttering a sound.

The alarm called her servants to the spot. They beheld her dumb, wildly gazing, and gesticulating in a way that indicated frenzy. She made no resistance to their efforts, but permitted them to carry her back to her own chamber. Sarah called upon her to speak, and to explain the cause of these appearances; but the shock which she had endured seemed to have irretrievably destroyed her powers of utterance.

The terrors of the affectionate Sarah were increased. She kneeled by the bedside of her mistress, and, with streaming eyes, besought the unhappy lady to compose herself. Perhaps the sight of weeping in another possessed a sympathetic influence, or nature had made provision for this salutary change. However that be, a torrent of tears now came to her succour, and rescued her from a paroxysm of insanity which its longer continuance might have set beyond the reach of cure.

Meanwhile, a glance at his master's countenance made Fabian fully acquainted with the nature of the scene. The ghastly visage of Mr. Dudley showed that he was dead, and that he had died in some terrific and mysterious manner. As soon as this faithful servant recovered from surprise, the first expedient which his ingenuity suggested was to fly with tidings of this event to Mr. Melbourne. That gentleman instantly obeyed the summons. With the power of weeping, Constantia recovered the power of reflection. This, for a time, served her only as a medium of anguish. Melbourne mingled his tears with hers, and endeavoured, by suitable remonstrances, to revive her fortitude.

The filial passion is perhaps instinctive to man; but its energy is modified by various circumstances. Every event in the life of Constantia contributed to heighten this passion beyond customary bounds. In the habit of perpetual attendance on her father, of deriving from him her knowledge, and sharing with him the hourly fruits of observation and reflection, his existence seemed blended with her own. There was no other whose concurrence and council she could claim, with whom a domestic and uninterrupted alliance could be maintained. The only bond of consanguinity was loosened, the only prop of friendship was taken away.

Others, perhaps, would have observed that her father's existence had been merely a source of obstruction and perplexity; that she had hitherto acted by her own wisdom, and would find, hereafter, less difficulty in her choice of schemes, and fewer impediments to the execution. These reflections occurred not to her. This disaster had increased, to an insupportable degree, the vacancy and dreariness of her existence. The face she was habituated to behold had disappeared forever; the voice whose mild and affecting tones had so long been familiar to her ears was hushed into eternal silence. The felicity to which she clung was ravished away; nothing remained to hinder her from sinking into utter despair.

The first transports of grief having subsided, a source of consolation seemed to be opened in the belief that her father had only changed one form of being for another; that he still lived to be the guardian of her peace and honour, to enter the recesses of her thought, to forewarn her of evil and invite her to good. She grasped at these images with eagerness, and fostered them as the only solaces of her calamity. They were not adapted to inspire her with cheerfulness, but they sublimed her sensations, and added an inexplicable fascination to sorrow.

It was unavoidable sometimes to reflect upon the nature of that death which had occurred. Tokens were sufficiently apparent that outward violence had been the cause. Who could be the performer of so black a deed, by what motives he was guided, were topics of fruitless conjecture. She mused upon this subject, not from the thirst of vengeance, but from a mournful curiosity. Had the perpetrator stood before her and challenged retribution, she would not have lifted a finger to accuse or to punish. The evil already endured left her no power to concert and execute projects for extending that evil to others. Her mind was unnerved, and recoiled with loathing from considerations of abstract justice, or political utility, when they prompted to the prosecution of the murderer.

Melbourne was actuated by different views, but on this subject he was painfully bewildered. Mr. Dudley's deportment to his servants and neighbours was gentle and humane. He had no dealings with the trafficking or labouring part of mankind. The fund which supplied his cravings of necessity or habit was his daughter's. His recreations and employments were harmless and lonely. The evil purpose was limited to his death, for his chamber was exactly in the same state in which negligent security had left it. No midnight footstep or voice, no unbarred door or lifted window, afforded tokens of the presence or traces of the entrance or flight of the assassin.

The meditations of Constantia, however, could not fail in some of their circuities to encounter the image of Craig. His agency in the impoverishment of her father, and in the scheme by which she had like to have been loaded with the penalties of forgery, was of an impervious and unprecedented kind. Motives were unveiled by time, in some degree accounting for his treacherous proceeding; but there was room to suppose an inborn propensity to mischief. Was he not the author of this new evil? His motives and his means were equally inscrutable, but their inscrutability might flow from her own defects in discernment and knowledge, and time might supply her defects in this as in former instances.

These images were casual. The causes of the evil were seldom contemplated. Her mind was rarely at liberty to wander from reflection on her irremediable loss. Frequently, when confused by distressful recollections, she would detect herself going to her father's chamber. Often his well-known accents would ring in her ears, and the momentary impulse would be to answer his calls. Her reluctance to sit down to her meals without her usual companion could scarcely be surmounted.

In this state of mind, the image of the only friend who survived, or whose destiny, at least, was doubtful, occurred to her. She sunk into fits of deeper abstraction and dissolved away in tears of more agonizing tenderness. A week after her father's interment, she shut herself up in her chamber, to torment herself with fruitless remembrances. The name of Sophia Westwyn was pronounced, and the ditty that solemnized their parting was sung. Now, more than formerly, she became sensible of the loss of that portrait which had been deposited in the hands of M'Crea as a pledge. As soon as her change of fortune had supplied her with the means of redeeming it, she hastened to M'Crea for that end. To her unspeakable disappointment, he was absent from the city; he had taken a long journey, and the exact period of his return could not be ascertained. His clerks refused to deliver the picture, or even, by searching, to discover whether it was still in their master's possession. This application had frequently and lately been repeated, but without success; M'Crea had not yet returned, and his family were equally in the dark as to the day on which his return might be expected.

She determined, on this occasion, to renew her visit. Her incessant disappointments had almost extinguished hope, and she made inquiries at his door, with a faltering accent and sinking heart. These emotions were changed into surprise and delight, when answer was made that he had just arrived. She was instantly conducted into his presence.

The countenance of M'Crea easily denoted that his visitant was by no means acceptable. There was a mixture of embarrassment and sullenness in his air, which was far from being diminished when the purpose of this visit was explained. Constantia reminded him of the offer and acceptance of this pledge, and of the conditions with which the transaction was accompanied.

He acknowledged, with some hesitation, that a promise had been given to retain the pledge until it were in her power to redeem it; but the long delay, the urgency of his own wants, and particularly the ill treatment which he conceived himself to have suffered in the transaction respecting the forged note, had, in his own opinion, absolved him from this promise. He had therefore sold the picture to a goldsmith, for as much as the gold about it was worth.

This information produced, in the heart of Constantia, a contest between indignation and sorrow, that for a time debarred her from speech. She stifled the anger that was, at length, rising to her lips, and calmly inquired to whom the picture had been sold.

M'Crea answered that for his part he had little dealings in gold and silver, but every thing of that kind which fell to his share he transacted with Mr. D——. This person was one of the most eminent of his profession. His character and place of abode were universally known. Tho only expedient that remained was to apply to him, and to ascertain, forthwith, the destiny of the picture. It was too probable that, when separated from its case, the portrait was thrown away or destroyed, as a mere encumbrance, but the truth was too momentous to be made the sport of mere probability. She left the house of M'Crea, and hastened to that of the goldsmith.

The circumstance was easily recalled to his remembrance. It was true that such a picture had been offered for sale, and that he had purchased it. The workmanship was curious, and he felt unwilling to destroy it. He therefore hung it up in his shop and indulged the hope that a purchaser would some time be attracted by the mere beauty of the toy.

Constantia's hopes were revived by these tidings, and she earnestly inquired if it were still in his possession.

"No. A young gentleman had entered his shop some months before: the picture had caught his fancy, and he had given a price which the artist owned he should not have demanded, had he not been encouraged by the eagerness which the gentleman betrayed to possess it."

"Who was this gentleman? Had there been any previous acquaintance between them? What was his name, his profession, and where was he to be found?"

"Really," the goldsmith answered, "he was ignorant respecting all those particulars. Previously to this purchase, the gentleman had sometimes visited his shop; but he did not recollect to have since seen him. He was unacquainted with his name and his residence."

"What appeared to be his motives for purchasing this picture?"

"The customer appeared highly pleased with it. Pleasure, rather than surprise, seemed to be produced by the sight of it. If I were permitted to judge," continued the artist, "I should imagine that the young man was acquainted with the original. To say the truth, I hinted as much at the time, and I did not see that he discouraged the supposition. Indeed, I cannot conceive how the picture could otherwise have gained any value in his eyes."

This only heightened the eagerness of Constantia to trace the footsteps of the youth. It was obvious to suppose some communication or connection between her friend and this purchaser. She repeated her inquiries, and the goldsmith, after some consideration, said, "Why, on second thoughts, I seem to have some notion of having seen a figure like that of my customer go into a lodging-house in Front Street, some time before I met with him at my shop."

The situation of this house being satisfactorily described, and the artist being able to afford her no further information, except as to stature and guise, she took her leave. There were two motives impelling her to prosecute her search after this person,—the desire of regaining this portrait and of procuring tidings of her friend. Involved as she was in ignorance, it was impossible to conjecture how far this incident would be subservient to these inestimable purposes. To procure an interview with this stranger was the first measure which prudence suggested.

She knew not his name or his person. He was once seen entering a lodging-house. Thither she must immediately repair; but how to introduce herself, how to describe the person of whom she was in search, she knew not. She was beset with embarrassments and difficulties. While her attention was entangled by these, she proceeded unconsciously on her way, and stopped not until she reached the mansion that had been described. Here she paused to collect her thoughts.

She found no relief in deliberation. Every moment added to her perplexity and indecision. Irresistibly impelled by her wishes, she at length, in a mood that partook of desperate, advanced to the door and knocked. The summons was immediately obeyed by a woman of decent appearance. A pause ensued, which Constantia at length terminated by a request to see the mistress of the house.

The lady courteously answered that she was the person, and immediately ushered her visitant into an apartment. Constantia being seated, the lady waited for the disclosure of her message. To prolong the silence was only to multiply embarrassments. She reverted to the state of her feelings, and saw that they flowed from inconsistency and folly. One vigorous effort was sufficient to restore her to composure and self-command.

She began with apologizing for a visit unpreceded by an introduction. The object of her inquiries was a person with whom it was of the utmost moment that she should procure a meeting, but whom, by an unfortunate concurrence of circumstances, she was unable to describe by the usual incidents of name and profession. Her knowledge was confined to his external appearance, and to the probability of his being an inmate of this house at the beginning of the year. She then proceeded to describe his person and dress.

"It is true," said the lady; "such a one as you describe has boarded in this house. His name was Martynne. I have good reason to remember him, for he lived with me three months, and then left the country without paying for his board."

"He has gone, then?" said Constantia, greatly discouraged by these tidings.

"Yes. He was a man of specious manners and loud pretensions. He came from England, bringing with him forged recommendatory letters, and, after passing from one end of the country to the other, contracting debts which he never paid and making bargains which he never fulfilled, he suddenly disappeared. It is likely that he has returned to Europe."

"Had he no kindred, no friends, no companions?"

"He found none here. He made pretences to alliances in England, which better information has, I believe, since shown to be false."

This was the sum of the information procurable from this source. Constantia was unable to conceal her chagrin. These symptoms were observed by the lady, whose curiosity was awakened in turn. Questions were obliquely started, inviting Constantia to a disclosure of her thoughts. No advantage would arise from confidence, and the guest, after a few minutes of abstraction and silence, rose to take her leave.

During this conference, some one appeared to be negligently sporting with the keys of a harpsichord, in the next apartment. The notes were too irregular and faint to make a forcible impression on the ear. In the present state of her mind, Constantia was merely conscious of the sound, in the intervals of conversation. Having arisen from her seat, her anxiety to obtain some information that might lead to the point she wished made her again pause. She endeavoured to invent some new interrogatory better suited to her purpose than those which had already been employed. A silence on both sides ensued.

During this interval, the unseen musician suddenly refrained from rambling, and glided into notes of some refinement and complexity. The cadence was aerial; but a thunderbolt, falling at her feet, would not have communicated a more visible shock to the senses of Constantia. A glance that denoted a tumult of soul bordering on distraction was now fixed upon the door that led into the room from whence the harmony proceeded. Instantly the cadence was revived, and some accompanying voice was heard to warble,—

> "Ah! far beyond this world of woes
> We meet to part,—to part no more."

Joy and grief, in their sudden onset and their violent extremes, approach so nearly in their influence on human beings as scarce to be distinguished. Constantia's frame was still enfeebled by her recent distresses. The torrent of emotion was too abrupt and too vehement. Her faculties were overwhelmed, and she sunk upon the floor motionless and without sense, but not till she had faintly articulated,—

"My God! My God! This is a joy unmerited and too great."

CHAPTER IV.

I must be forgiven if I now introduce myself on the stage. Sophia Westwyn is the friend of Constantia, and the writer of this narrative. So far as my fate was connected with that of my friend, it is worthy to be known. That connection has constituted the joy and misery of my existence, and has prompted me to undertake this task.

I assume no merit from the desire of knowledge and superiority to temptation. There is little of which I can boast; but that little I derived, instrumentally, from Constantia. Poor as my attainments are, it is to her that I am indebted for them all. Life itself was the gift of her father, but my virtue and felicity are her gifts. That I am neither indigent nor profligate, flows from her bounty.

I am not unaware of the divine superintendence,—of the claims upon my gratitude and service which pertain to my God. I know that all physical and moral agents are merely instrumental to the purpose that he wills; but, though the great Author of being and felicity must not be forgotten, it is neither possible nor just to overlook the claims upon our love with which our fellow-beings are invested.

The supreme love does not absorb, but chastens and enforces, all subordinate affections. In proportion to the rectitude of my perceptions and the ardour of my piety, must I clearly discern and fervently love the excellence discovered in my fellow-beings, and industriously promote their improvement and felicity.

From my infancy to my seventeenth year, I lived in the house of Mr. Dudley. On the day of my birth I was deserted by my mother. Her temper was more akin to that of tigress than woman. Yet that is unjust; for beasts cherish their offspring. No natures but human are capable of that depravity which makes insensible to the claims of innocence and helplessness.

But let me not recall her to memory. Have I not enough of sorrow? Yet to omit my causes of disquiet, the unprecedented forlornness of my condition, and the persecutions of an unnatural parent, would be to leave my character a problem, and the sources of my love of Miss Dudley unexplored. Yet I must not dwell upon that complication of iniquities, that savage ferocity and unextinguishable hatred of me, which characterized my unhappy mother.

I was not safe under the protection of Mr. Dudley, nor happy in the caresses of his daughter. My mother asserted the privilege of that relation: she laboured for years to obtain the control of my person and actions, to snatch me from a peaceful and chaste asylum, and detain me in her own house, where, indeed, I should not have been in want of raiment and food; but where—

O my mother! Let me not dishonour thy name! Yet it is not in my power to enhance thy infamy. Thy crimes, unequalled as they were, were perhaps expiated by thy penitence. Thy offences are too well known; but perhaps they who witnessed thy freaks of intoxication, thy defiance of public shame, the enormity of thy pollutions, the infatuation that made thee glory in the pursuit of a loathsome and detestable trade, may be strangers to the remorse and the abstinence which accompanied the close of thy ignominious life.

For ten years was my peace incessantly molested by the menaces or machinations of my mother. The longer she meditated my destruction, the more tenacious of her purpose and indefatigable in her efforts she became. That my mind was harassed with perpetual alarms was not enough. The fame and tranquillity of Mr. Dudley and his daughter were hourly assailed. My mother resigned herself to the impulses of malignity and rage. Headlong passions, and a vigorous though perverted understanding, were hers. Hence, her stratagems to undermine the reputation of my protector, and to bereave him of domestic comfort, were subtle and profound. Had she not herself been careless of that good which she endeavoured to wrest from others, her artifices could scarcely have been frustrated.

In proportion to the hazard which accrued to my protector and friend, the more ardent their zeal in my defence and their affection for my person became. They watched over me with ineffable solicitude. At all hours and in every occupation, I was the companion of Constantia. All my wants were supplied in the same proportion as hers. The tenderness of Mr. Dudley seemed equally divided between us. I partook of his instructions, and the means of every intellectual and personal gratification were lavished upon me.

The speed of my mother's career in infamy was at length slackened. She left New York, which had long been the theatre of her vices. Actuated by a now caprice, she determined to travel through the Southern States. Early indulgence was the cause of her ruin, but her parents had given her the embellishments of a fashionable education. She delighted to assume all parts, and personate the most opposite characters. She now resolved to carry a new name, and the mask of virtue, into scenes hitherto unvisited.

She journeyed as far as Charleston. Here she met an inexperienced youth, lately arrived from England, and in possession of an ample fortune. Her speciousness and artifices seduced him into a precipitate marriage. Her true character, however, could not be long concealed by herself, and her vices had been too conspicuous for her long to escape recognition. Her husband was infatuated by her blandishments. To abandon her, or to contemplate her depravity with unconcern, were equally beyond his power. Romantic in his sentiments, his fortitude was unequal to his disappointments, and he speedily sunk into the grave. By a similar refinement in generosity, he bequeathed to her his property.

With this accession of wealth, she returned to her ancient abode. The mask lately worn seemed preparing to be thrown aside, and her profligate habits to be resumed with more eagerness than ever; but an unexpected and total revolution was effected, by the exhortations of a Methodist divine. Her heart seemed, on a sudden, to be remoulded, her vices and the abettors of them were abjured, she shut out the intrusions of society, and prepared to expiate, by the rigours of abstinence and the bitterness of tears, the offences of her past life.

In this, as in her former career, she was unacquainted with restraint and moderation. Her remorses gained strength in proportion as she cherished them. She brooded over the images of her guilt, till the possibility of forgiveness and remission disappeared. Her treatment of her daughter and her husband constituted the chief source of her torment. Her awakened conscience refused her a momentary respite from its persecutions. Her thoughts became, by rapid degrees, tempestuous and gloomy, and it was at length evident that her condition was maniacal.

In this state, she was to me an object, no longer of terror, but compassion. She was surrounded by hirelings, devoid of personal attachment, and anxious only to convert her misfortunes to their own advantage. This evil it was my duty to obviate. My presence, for a time, only enhanced the vehemence of her malady; but at length it was only by my attendance and soothing that she was diverted from the fellest purposes. Shocking execrations and outrages, resolutions and efforts to destroy herself and those around her, were sure to take place in my absence. The moment I appeared before her, her fury abated, her gesticulations were becalmed, and her voice exerted only in incoherent and pathetic lamentations.

These scenes, though so different from those which I had formerly been condemned to witness, were scarcely less excruciating. The friendship of Constantia Dudley was my only consolation. She took up her abode with me, and shared with me every disgustful and perilous office which my mother's insanity prescribed.

Of this consolation, however, it was my fate to be bereaved. My mother's state was deplorable, and no remedy hitherto employed was efficacious. A voyage to England was conceived likely to benefit, by change of temperature and scenes, and by the opportunity it would afford of trying the superior skill of English physicians. This scheme, after various struggles on my part, was adopted. It was detestable to my imagination, because it severed me from that friend in whose existence mine was involved, and without whose participation knowledge lost its attractions and society became a torment.

The prescriptions of my duty could not be disguised or disobeyed, and we parted. A mutual engagement was formed to record every sentiment and relate every event that happened in the life of either, and no opportunity of communicating information was to be omitted. This engagement was punctually performed on my part. I sought out every method of conveyance to my friend, and took infinite pains to procure tidings from her; but all were ineffectual.

My mother's malady declined, but was succeeded by a pulmonary disease, which threatened her speedy destruction. By the restoration of her understanding, the purpose of her voyage was obtained, and my impatience to return, which the inexplicable and ominous silence of my friend daily increased, prompted me to exert all my powers of persuasion to induce her to revisit America.

My mother's frenzy was a salutary crisis in her moral history. She looked back upon her past conduct with unspeakable loathing, but this retrospect only invigorated her devotion and her virtue; but the thought of returning to the scene of her unhappiness and infamy could not be endured. Besides, life, in her eyes, possessed considerable attractions, and her physicians flattered her with recovery from her present disease, if she would change the atmosphere of England for that of Languedoc and Naples.

I followed her with murmurs and reluctance. To desert her in her present critical state would have been inhuman. My mother's aversions and attachments, habits and views, were dissonant with my own. Conformity of sentiments and impressions of maternal tenderness did not exist to bind us to each other. My attendance was assiduous, but it was the sense of duty that rendered my attendance a supportable task.

Her decay was eminently gradual. No time seemed to diminish her appetite for novelty and change. During three years we traversed every part of France, Switzerland, and Italy. I could not but attend to surrounding scenes, and mark the progress of the mighty revolution, whose effects, like agitation in a fluid, gradually spread from Paris, the centre, over the face of the neighbouring kingdoms; but there passed not a day or an hour in which the image of Constantia was not recalled, in which the most pungent regrets were not felt at the inexplicable silence which had been observed by her, and the most vehement longings indulged to return to my native country. My exertions to ascertain her condition by indirect means, by interrogating natives of America with whom I chanced to meet, were unwearied, but, for a long period, ineffectual.

During this pilgrimage, Rome was thrice visited. My mother's indisposition was hastening to a crisis, and she formed the resolution of closing her life at the bottom of Vesuvius. We stopped, for the sake of a few days' repose, at Rome. On the morning after our arrival, I accompanied some friends to view the public edifices. Casting my eyes over the vast and ruinous interior of the Coliseum, my attention was fixed by the figure of a young man whom, after a moment's pause, I recollected to have seen in the streets of New York. At a distance from home, mere community of country is no inconsiderable bond of affection. The social spirit prompts us to cling even to inanimate objects, when they remind us of ancient fellowships and juvenile attachments.

A servant was despatched to summon this stranger, who recognised a countrywoman with a pleasure equal to that which I had received. On nearer view, this person, whose name was Courtland, did not belie my favourable prepossessions. Our intercourse was soon established on a footing of confidence and intimacy.

The destiny of Constantia was always uppermost in my thoughts. This person's acquaintance was originally sought chiefly in the hope of obtaining from him some information respecting my friend. On inquiry, I discovered that he had left his native city seven months after me. Having tasked his recollection and compared a number of facts, the name of Dudley at length recurred to him. He had casually heard the history of Craig's imposture and its consequences. These were now related as circumstantially as a memory occupied by subsequent incidents enabled him. The tale had been told to him, in a domestic circle which he was accustomed to frequent, by the person who purchased Mr. Dudley's lute and restored it to its previous owner on the conditions formerly mentioned.

This tale filled me with anguish and doubt. My impatience to search out this unfortunate girl, and share with her her sorrows or relieve them, was anew excited by this mournful intelligence. That Constantia Dudley was reduced to beggary was too abhorrent to my feelings to receive credit; yet the sale of her father's property, comprising even his furniture and clothing, seemed to prove that she had fallen even to this depth. This enabled me in some degree to account for her silence. Her generous spirit would induce her to conceal misfortunes from her friend which no communication would alleviate. It was possible that she had selected some new abode, and that, in consequence, the letters I had written, and which amounted to volumes, had never reached her hands.

My mother's state would not suffer me to obey the impulse of my heart. Her frame was verging towards dissolution. Courtland's engagements allowed him to accompany us to Naples, and here the long series of my mother's pilgrimages closed in death. Her obsequies were no sooner performed, than I determined to set out on my long-projected voyage. My mother's property, which, in consequence of her decease, devolved upon me, was not inconsiderable. There is scarcely any good so dear to a rational being as competence. I was not unacquainted with its benefits, but this acquisition was valuable to mo chiefly as it enabled me to reunite my fate to that of Constantia.

Courtland was my countryman and friend. He was destitute of fortune, and had been led to Europe partly by the spirit of adventure, and partly on a mercantile project. He had made sale of his property on advantageous terms, in the ports of France, and resolved to consume the produce in examining this scene of heroic exploits and memorable revolutions. His slender stock, though frugally and even parsimoniously administered, was nearly exhausted; and, at the time of our meeting at Rome, he was making reluctant preparations to return.

Sufficient opportunity was afforded us, in an unrestrained and domestic intercourse of three months, which succeeded our Roman interview, to gain a knowledge of each other. There was that conformity of tastes and views between us which could scarcely fail, at an age and in a situation like ours, to give birth to tenderness. My resolution to hasten to America was peculiarly unwelcome to my friend. He had offered to be my companion, but this offer my regard to his interest obliged me to decline; but I was willing to compensate him for this denial, as well as to gratify my own heart, by an immediate marriage.

So long a residence in England and Italy had given birth to friendships and connections of the dearest kind. I had no view but to spend my life with Courtland, in the midst of my maternal kindred, who were English. A voyage to America and reunion with Constantia were previously indispensable; but I hoped that my friend might be prevailed upon, and that her disconnected situation would permit her to return with me to Europe. If this end could not be accomplished, it was my inflexible purpose to live and die with her. Suitably to this arrangement, Courtland was to repair to London, and wait patiently till I should be able to rejoin him there, or to summon him to meet me in America.

A week after my mother's death, I became a wife, and embarked the next day, at Naples, in a Ragusan ship, destined for New York. The voyage was tempestuous and tedious. The vessel was necessitated to make a short stay at

Toulon. The state of that city, however, then in possession of the English and besieged by the revolutionary forces, was adverse to commercial views. Happily, we resumed our voyage on the day previous to that on which the place was evacuated by the British. Our seasonable departure rescued us from witnessing a scene of horrors of which the history of former wars furnishes us with few examples.

A cold and boisterous navigation awaited us. My palpitations and inquietudes augmented as we approached the American coast. I shall not forget the sensations which I experienced on the sight of the Beacon at Sandy Hook. It was first seen at midnight, in a stormy and beclouded atmosphere, emerging from the waves, whose fluctuation allowed it, for some time, to be visible only by fits. This token of approaching land affected me as much as if I had reached the threshold of my friend's dwelling.

At length we entered the port, and I viewed, with high-raised but inexplicable feelings, objects with which I had been from infancy familiar. The flagstaff erected on the Battery recalled to my imagination the pleasures of the evening and morning walks which I had taken on that spot with the lost Constantia. The dream was fondly cherished, that the figure which I saw loitering along the terrace was hers.

On disembarking, I gazed at every female passenger, in hope that it was she whom I sought. An absence of three years had obliterated from my memory none of the images which attended me on my departure.

CHAPTER V.

After a night of repose rather than of sleep, I began the search after my friend. I went to the house which the Dudleys formerly inhabited, and which had been the asylum of my infancy. It was now occupied by strangers, by whom no account could be given of its former tenants. I obtained directions to the owner of the house. He was equally unable to satisfy my curiosity. The purchase had been made at a public sale, and terms had been settled, not with Dudley, but with the sheriff.

It is needless to say that the history of Craig's imposture and its consequences were confirmed by every one who resided at that period in New York. The Dudleys were well remembered, and their disappearance, immediately after their fall, had been generally noticed; but whither they had retired was a problem which no one was able to solve.

This evasion was strange. By what motives the Dudleys were induced to change their ancient abode could be vaguely guessed. My friend's grandfather was a native of the West Indies. Descendants of the same stock still resided in Tobago. They might be affluent, and to them it was possible that Mr. Dudley, in this change of fortune, had betaken himself for relief. This was a mournful expedient, since it would raise a barrier between my friend and myself scarcely to be surmounted.

Constantia's mother was stolen by Mr. Dudley from a convent at Amiens. There were no affinities, therefore, to draw them to France. Her grandmother was a native of Baltimore, of a family of some note, by name Ridgeley. This family might still exist, and have either afforded an asylum to the Dudleys, or, at least, be apprized of their destiny. It was obvious to conclude that they no longer existed within the precincts of New York. A journey to Baltimore was the next expedient.

This journey was made in the depth of winter, and by the speediest conveyance. I made no more than a day's sojourn in Philadelphia. The epidemic by which that city had been lately ravaged, I had not heard of till my arrival in America. Its devastations were then painted to my fancy in the most formidable colours. A few months only had elapsed since its extinction, and I expected to see numerous marks of misery and depopulation.

To my no small surprise, however, no vestiges of this calamity were to be discerned. All houses were open, all streets thronged, and all faces thoughtless or busy. The arts and the amusements of life seemed as sedulously cultivated as ever. Little did I then think what had been, and what at that moment was, the condition of my friend. I stopped for the sake of respite from fatigue, and did not, therefore, pass much time in the streets. Perhaps, had I walked seasonably abroad, we might have encountered each other, and thus have saved ourselves from a thousand anxieties.

At Baltimore I made myself known, without the formality of introduction, to the Ridgeleys. They acknowledged their relationship to Mr. Dudley, but professed absolute ignorance of his fate. Indirect intercourse only had been maintained, formerly, by Dudley with his mother's kindred. They had heard of his misfortune a twelvemonth after it happened; but what measures had been subsequently pursued, their kinsman had not thought proper to inform them.

The failure of this expedient almost bereft me of hope. Neither my own imagination nor the Ridgeleys could suggest any new mode by which my purpose was likely to be accomplished. To leave America without obtaining the end of my visit could not be thought of without agony; and yet the continuance of my stay promised me no relief from my uncertainties.

On this theme I ruminated without ceasing. I recalled every conversation and incident of former times, and sought in them a clue by which my present conjectures might be guided. One night, immersed alone in my chamber, my thoughts were thus employed. My train of meditation was, on this occasion, new. From the review of particulars from which no satisfaction had hitherto been gained, I passed to a vague and comprehensive retrospect.

Mr. Dudley's early life, his profession of a painter, his zeal in this pursuit, and his reluctance to quit it, were remembered. Would he not revert to this profession when other means of subsistence were gone? It is true, similar obstacles with those which had formerly occasioned his resort to a different path existed at present, and no painter of his name was to be found in Philadelphia, Baltimore, or New York. But would it not occur to him, that the patronage denied to his skill by the frugal and unpolished habits of his countrymen might, with more probability of success, be sought from the opulence and luxury of London? Nay, had he not once affirmed, in my hearing, that, if he ever were reduced to poverty, this was the method he would pursue?

This conjecture was too bewitching to be easily dismissed. Every new reflection augmented its force. I was suddenly raised by it from the deepest melancholy to the region of lofty and gay hopes. Happiness, of which I had begun to imagine myself irretrievably bereft, seemed once more to approach within my reach. Constantia would not only be found, but be met in the midst of those comforts which her father's skill could not fail to procure, and on that very stage where I most desired to encounter her. Mr. Dudley had many friends and associates of his youth in London. Filial duty had repelled their importunities to fix his abode in Europe, when summoned home by his father. On his father's death these solicitations had been renewed, but were disregarded for reasons which he, afterwards, himself confessed were fallacious. That they would a third time be preferred, and would regulate his conduct, seemed to me incontestable.

I regarded with wonder and deep regret the infatuation that had hitherto excluded these images from my understanding and my memory. How many dangers and toils had I endured since my embarkation at Naples, to the present moment! How many lingering minutes had I told since my first interview with Courtland! All were owing to my own stupidity. Had my present thoughts been seasonably suggested, I might long since have been restored to the embraces of my friend, without the necessity of an hour's separation from my husband.

These were evils to be repaired as far as it was possible. Nothing now remained but to procure a passage to Europe. For this end diligent inquiries were immediately set on foot. A vessel was found, which, in a few weeks, would set out upon the voyage. Having bespoken a conveyance, it was incumbent on me to sustain with patience the unwelcome delay.

Meanwhile, my mind, delivered from the dejection and perplexities that lately haunted it, was capable of some attention to surrounding objects. I marked the peculiarities of manners and language in my new abode, and studied the effects which a political and religious system so opposite to that with which I had conversed in Italy and Switzerland had produced. I found that the difference between Europe and America lay chiefly in this:—that, in the former, all things tended to extremes, whereas, in the latter, all things tended to the same level. Genius, and virtue, and happiness, on these shores, were distinguished by a sort of mediocrity. Conditions were less unequal, and men were strangers to the heights of enjoyment and the depths of misery to which the inhabitants of Europe are accustomed.

I received friendly notice and hospitable treatment from the Ridgeleys. These people were mercantile and plodding in their habits. I found in their social circle little exercise for the sympathies of my heart, and willingly accepted their aid to enlarge the sphere of my observation.

About a week before my intended embarkation, and when suitable preparation had been made for that event, a lady arrived in town, who was cousin to my Constantia. She had frequently been mentioned in favourable terms in my hearing. She had passed her life in a rural abode with her father, who cultivated his own domain, lying forty miles from Baltimore.

On an offer being made to introduce us to each other, I consented to know one whose chief recommendation in my eyes consisted in her affinity to Constantia Dudley. I found an artless and attractive female, unpolished and undepraved by much intercourse with mankind. At first sight, I was powerfully struck by the resemblance of her features to those of my friend, which sufficiently denoted their connection with a common stock.

The first interview afforded mutual satisfaction. On our second meeting, discourse insensibly led to the mention of Miss Dudley, and of the design which had brought me to America. She was deeply affected by the earnestness with which I expatiated on her cousin's merits, and by the proofs which my conduct had given of unlimited attachment.

I dwelt immediately on the measures which I had hitherto ineffectually pursued to trace her footsteps, and detailed the grounds of my present belief that we should meet in London. During this recital, my companion sighed and wept. When I finished my tale, her tears, instead of ceasing, flowed with new vehemence. This appearance excited some surprise, and I ventured to ask the cause of her grief.

"Alas!" she replied, "I am personally a stranger to my cousin, but her character has been amply displayed to me by one who knew her well. I weep to think how much she has suffered. How much excellence we have lost!"

"Nay," said I, "all her sufferings will, I hope, be compensated, and I by no means consider her as lost. If my search in London be unsuccessful, then shall I indeed despair."

"Despair, then, already," said my sobbing companion, "for your search will be unsuccessful. How I feel for your disappointment! but it cannot be known too soon. My cousin is dead!"

These tidings were communicated with tokens of sincerity and sorrow that left me no room to doubt that they were believed by the relater. My own emotions were suspended till interrogations had obtained a knowledge of her reasons for crediting this fatal event, and till she had explained the time and manner of her death. A friend of Miss Ridgeley's father had witnessed the devastations of the yellow fever in Philadelphia. He was apprized of the relationship that subsisted between his friend and the Dudleys. He gave a minute and circumstantial account of the arts of Craig. He mentioned the removal of my friends to Philadelphia, their obscure and indigent life, and, finally, their falling victims to the pestilence.

He related the means by which he became apprized of their fate, and drew a picture of their death, surpassing all that imagination can conceive of shocking and deplorable. The quarter where they lived was nearly desolate. Their house was shut up, and, for a time, imagined to be uninhabited. Some suspicions being awakened in those who superintended the burial of the dead, the house was entered, and the father and child discovered to be dead. The former was stretched upon his wretched pallet, while the daughter was found on the floor of the lower room, in a state that denoted the sufferance not only of disease, but of famine.

This tale was false. Subsequent discoveries proved this to be a detestable artifice of Craig, who, stimulated by incurable habits, had invented these disasters, for the purpose of enhancing the opinion of his humanity and of furthering his views on the fortune and daughter of Mr. Ridgeley.

Its falsehood, however, I had as yet no means of ascertaining. I received it as true, and at once dismissed all my claims upon futurity. All hope of happiness, in this mutable and sublunary scene, was fled. Nothing remained but to join my friend in a world where woes are at an end and virtue finds recompense. "Surely," said I, "there will some time be a close to calamity and discord. To those whose lives have been blameless, but harassed by

33

inquietudes to which not their own but the errors of others have given birth, a fortress will hereafter be assigned unassailable by change, impregnable to sorrow.

"O my ill-fated Constantia! I will live to cherish thy remembrance, and to emulate thy virtue. I will endure the privation of thy friendship and the vicissitudes that shall befall me, and draw my consolation and courage from the foresight of no distant close to this terrestrial scene, and of ultimate and everlasting union with thee."

This consideration, though it kept me from confusion and despair, could not, but with the healing aid of time, render me tranquil or strenuous. My strength was unequal to the struggle of my passions. The ship in which I engaged to embark could not wait for my restoration to health, and I was left behind.

Mary Ridgeley was artless and affectionate. She saw that her society was dearer to me than that of any other, and was therefore seldom willing to leave my chamber. Her presence, less on her own account than by reason of her personal resemblance and her affinity by birth to Constantia, was a powerful solace.

I had nothing to detain me longer in America. I was anxious to change my present lonely state, for the communion of those friends in England, and the performance of those duties, which were left to me. I was informed that a British packet would shortly sail from New York. My frame was sunk into greater weakness than I had felt at any former period; and I conceived that to return to New York by water was more commodious than to perform the journey by land.

This arrangement was likewise destined to be disappointed. One morning I visited, according to my custom, Mary Ridgeley. I found her in a temper somewhat inclined to gayety. She rallied me, with great archness, on the care with which I had concealed from her a tender engagement into which I had lately entered.

I supposed myself to comprehend her allusion, and therefore answered that accident, rather than design, had made me silent on the subject of marriage. She had hitherto known me by no appellation but Sophia Courtland. I had thought it needless to inform her that I was indebted for my name to my husband, Courtland being his name.

"All that," said my friend, "I know already. And so you sagely think that my knowledge goes no further than that? We are not bound to love our husbands longer than their lives. There is no crime, I believe, in referring the living to the dead; and most heartily do congratulate you on your present choice."

34

"What mean you? I confess, your discourse surpasses my comprehension."

At that moment the bell at the door rung a loud peal. Miss Ridgeley hastened down at this signal, saying, with much significance,—

"I am a poor hand at solving a riddle. Here comes one who, if I mistake not, will find no difficulty in clearing up your doubts."

Presently she came up, and said, with a smile of still greater archness, "Here is a young gentleman, a friend of mine, to whom I must have the pleasure of introducing you. He has come for the special purpose of solving my riddle." I attended her to the parlour without hesitation.

She presented me, with great formality, to a youth, whose appearance did not greatly prepossess me in favour of his judgement. He approached me with an air supercilious and ceremonious; but the moment he caught a glance at my face, he shrunk back, visibly confounded and embarrassed. A pause ensued, in which Miss Ridgeley had opportunity to detect the error into which she had been led by the vanity of this young man.

"How now, Mr. Martynne!" said my friend, in a tone of ridicule; "is it possible you do not know the lady who is the queen of your affections, the tender and indulgent fair one whose portrait you carry in your bosom, and whose image you daily and nightly bedew with your tears and kisses?"

Mr. Martynne's confusion, instead of being subdued by his struggle, only grew more conspicuous; and, after a few incoherent speeches and apologies, during which he carefully avoided encountering my eyes, he hastily departed.

I applied to my friend, with great earnestness, for an explanation of this scene. It seems that, in the course of conversation with him on the preceding day, he had suffered a portrait which hung at his breast to catch Miss Ridgeley's eye. On her betraying a desire to inspect it more nearly, he readily produced it. My image had been too well copied by the artist not to be instantly recognised.

She concealed her knowledge of the original, and, by questions well adapted to the purpose, easily drew from him confessions that this was the portrait of his mistress. He let fall sundry innuendoes and surmises, tending to impress her with a notion of the rank, fortune, and intellectual accomplishments of the nymph, and particularly of the doting fondness and measureless confidence with which she regarded him.

Her imperfect knowledge of my situation left her in some doubt as to the truth of these pretensions, and she was willing to ascertain the truth by bringing about an interview. To guard against evasions and artifice in the lover, she carefully concealed from him her knowledge of the original, and merely pretended that a friend of hers was far more beautiful than her whom this picture represented. She added, that she expected a visit from her friend the next morning, and was willing, by showing her to Mr. Martynne, to convince him how much he was mistaken in supposing the perfections of his mistress unrivalled.

CHAPTER VI.

Martynne, while ho expressed his confidence that the experiment would only confirm his triumph, readily assented to the proposal, and the interview above described took place, accordingly, the next morning. Had he not been taken by surprise, it is likely the address of a man who possessed no contemptible powers would have extricated him from some of his embarrassment.

That my portrait should be in the possession of one whom I had never before seen, and whose character and manners entitled him to no respect, was a source of some surprise. This mode of multiplying faces is extremely prevalent in this age, and was eminently characteristic of those with whom I had associated in different parts of Europe. The nature of my thoughts had modified my features into an expression which my friends were pleased to consider as a model for those who desired to personify the genius of suffering and resignation.

Hence, among those whose religion permitted their devotion to a picture of a female, the symbols of their chosen deity were added to features and shape that resembled mine. My own caprice, as well as that of others, always dictated a symbolical, and, in every new instance, a different accompaniment of this kind. Hence was offered the means of tracing the history of that picture which Martynne possessed.

It had been accurately examined by Miss Ridgeley, and her description of the frame in which it was placed instantly informed me that it was the same which, at our parting, I left in the possession of Constantia. My friend and myself were desirous of employing the skill of a Saxon painter, by name Eckstein. Each of us were drawn by him, she with the cincture of Venus, and I with the crescent of Dian. This symbol was still conspicuous on the brow of that image which Miss Ridgeley had examined, and served to identify the original proprietor.

This circumstance tended to confirm my fears that Constantia was dead, since that she would part with this picture during her life was not to be believed. It was of little moment to discover how it came into the hands of the present possessor. Those who carried her remains to the grave had probably torn it from her neck and afterwards disposed of it for money.

By whatever means, honest or illicit, it had been acquired by Martynne, it was proper that it should be restored to me. It was valuable to me, because it had been the property of one whom I loved, and it might prove highly injurious to my fame and my happiness, as the tool of this man's vanity and the attestor of his falsehood. I therefore wrote him a letter, acquainting him with my reasons for desiring the repossession of this picture, and offering a price for it at least double its value as a mere article of traffic. Martynne accepted the terms. He transmitted the picture, and with it a note, apologizing for the artifice of which he had been guilty, and mentioning, in order to justify his acceptance of the price which I had offered, that he had lately purchased it for an equal sum, of a goldsmith in Philadelphia.

This information suggested a new reflection. Constantia had engaged to preserve, for the use of her friend, copious and accurate memorials of her life. Copies of these were, on suitable occasions, to be transmitted to me during my residence abroad. These I had never received, but it was highly probable that her punctuality, in the performance of the first part of her engagement, had been equal to my own.

What, I asked, had become of these precious memorials? In the wreck of her property were these irretrievably engulfed? It was not probable that they had been wantonly destroyed. They had fallen, perhaps, into hands careless or unconscious of their value, or still lay, unknown and neglected, at the bottom of some closet or chest. Their recovery might be effected by vehement exertions, or by some miraculous accident. Suitable inquiries, carried on among those who were active in those scenes of calamity, might afford some clue by which the fate of the Dudleys, and the disposition of their property, might come into fuller light. These inquiries could be made only in Philadelphia, and thither, for that purpose, I now resolved to repair. There was still an interval of some weeks before the departure of the packet in which I proposed to embark.

Having returned to the capital, I devoted all my zeal to my darling project. My efforts, however, were without success. Those who administered charity and succour during that memorable season, and who survived, could remove none of my doubts, nor answer any of my inquiries. Innumerable tales, equally disastrous with those which Miss Ridgeley had heard, were related; but, for a considerable period, none of their circumstances were sufficiently accordant with the history of the Dudleys.

It is worthy of remark, in how many ways, and by what complexity of motives, human curiosity is awakened and knowledge obtained. By its connection with my darling purpose, every event in the history of this memorable pest was earnestly sought and deeply pondered. The powerful considerations which governed me made me slight those punctilious impediments which, in other circumstances, would have debarred me from intercourse with the immediate actors and observers. I found none who were unwilling to expatiate on this topic, or to communicate the knowledge they possessed. Their details were copious in particulars and vivid in minuteness. They exhibited the state of manners, the diversified effects of evil or heroic passions, and the endless forms which sickness and poverty assume in the obscure recesses of a commercial and populous city.

Some of these details are too precious to be lost. It is above all things necessary that we should be thoroughly acquainted with the condition of our fellow-beings. Justice and compassion are the fruit of knowledge. The misery that overspreads so large a part of mankind exists chiefly because those who are able to relieve it do not know that it exists. Forcibly to paint the evil, seldom fails to excite the virtue of the spectator and seduce him into wishes, at least, if not into exertions, of beneficence.

The circumstances in which I was placed were, perhaps, wholly singular. Hence, the knowledge I obtained was more comprehensive and authentic than was possessed by any one, even of the immediate actors or sufferers. This knowledge will not be useless to myself or to the world. The motives which dictated the present narrative will hinder me from relinquishing the pen till my fund of observation and experience be exhausted. Meanwhile, let me resume the thread of my tale.

The period allowed me before my departure was nearly expired, and my purpose seemed to be as far from its accomplishment as ever. One evening I visited a lady who was the widow of a physician whose disinterested exertions had cost him his life. She dwelt with pathetic earnestness on the particulars of her own distress, and listened with deep attention to the inquiries and doubts which I had laid before her.

After a pause of consideration, she said that an incident like that related by me she had previously heard from one of her friends, whose name she mentioned. This person was one of those whose office consisted in searching out the sufferers, and affording them unsought and unsolicited relief. She was offering to introduce me to this person, when he entered the apartment.

After the usual compliments, my friend led the conversation as I wished. Between Mr. Thompson's tale and that related to Miss Ridgeley there was an obvious resemblance. The sufferers resided in an obscure alley. They had shut themselves up from all intercourse with their neighbours, and had died, neglected and unknown. Mr. Thompson was vested with the superintendence of this district, and had passed the house frequently without suspicion of its being tenanted.

He was at length informed, by one of those who conducted a hearse, that he had seen the window in the upper story of this house lifted and a female show herself. It was night, and the hearseman chanced to be passing the door. He immediately supposed that the person stood in need of his services, and stopped.

This procedure was comprehended by the person at the window, who, leaning out, addressed him in a broken and feeble voice. She asked him why he had not taken a different route, and upbraided him for inhumanity in leading his noisy vehicle past her door. She wanted repose, but the ceaseless rumbling of his wheels would not allow her the sweet respite of a moment.

This invective was singular, and uttered in a voice which united the utmost degree of earnestness with a feebleness that rendered it almost inarticulate. The man was at a loss for a suitable answer. His pause only increased the impatience of the person at the window, who called upon him, in a still more anxious tone, to proceed, and entreated him to avoid this alley for the future.

He answered that he must come whenever the occasion called him; that three persons now lay dead in this alley, and that he must be expeditious in their removal; but that he would return as seldom and make as little noise as possible.

He was interrupted by new exclamations and upbraidings. These terminated in a burst of tears, and assertions that God and man were her enemies,—that they were determined to destroy her; but she trusted that the time would come when their own experience would avenge her wrongs, and teach them some compassion for the misery of others. Saying this, she shut the window with violence, and retired from it, sobbing with a vehemence that could be distinctly overheard by him in the street.

He paused for some time, listening when this passion should cease. The habitation was slight, and he imagined that he heard her traversing the floor. While he stayed, she continued to vent her anguish in exclamations and sighs and passionate weeping. It did not appear that any other person was within.

Mr. Thompson, being next day informed of these incidents, endeavoured to enter the house; but his signals, though loud and frequently repeated, being unnoticed, he was obliged to gain admission by violence. An old man, and a female lovely in the midst of emaciation and decay, were discovered without signs of life. The death of the latter appeared to have been very recent.

In examining the house, no traces of other inhabitants were to be found.

Nothing serviceable as food was discovered, but the remnants of mouldy bread scattered on a table. No information could be gathered from neighbours respecting the condition and name of these unfortunate people. They had taken possession of this house during the rage of this malady, and refrained from all communication with their neighbours.

There was too much resemblance between this and the story formerly heard, not to produce the belief that they related to the same persons. All that remained was to obtain directions to the proprietor of this dwelling, and exact from him all that he knew respecting his tenants.

I found in him a man of worth and affability. He readily related, that a man applied to him for the use of this house, and that the application was received. At the beginning of the pestilence, a numerous family inhabited this tenement, but had died in rapid succession. This new applicant was the first to apprize him of this circumstance, and appeared extremely anxious to enter on immediate possession.

It was intimated to him that danger would arise from the pestilential condition of the house. Unless cleansed and purified, disease would be unavoidably contracted. The inconvenience and hazard this applicant was willing to encounter, and, at length, hinted that no alternative was allowed him by his present landlord but to lie in the street or to procure some other abode.

"What was the external appearance of this person?"

"He was infirm, past the middle age, of melancholy aspect and indigent garb. A year had since elapsed, and more characteristic particulars had not been remarked, or were forgotten. The name had been mentioned, but, in the midst of more recent and momentous transactions, had vanished from remembrance. Dudley, or Dolby, or Hadley, seemed to approach more nearly than any other sounds."

Permission to inspect the house was readily granted. It had remained, since that period, unoccupied. The furniture and goods were scanty and wretched, and he did not care to endanger his safety by meddling with them. He believed that they had not been removed or touched.

I was insensible of any hazard which attended my visit, and, with the guidance of a servant, who felt as little apprehension as myself, hastened to the spot. I found nothing but tables and chairs. Clothing was nowhere to be seen. An earthen pot, without handle, and broken, stood upon the kitchen-hearth. No other implement or vessel for the preparation of food appeared.

These forlorn appearances were accounted for by the servant, by supposing the house to have been long since rifled of every thing worth the trouble of removal, by the villains who occupied the neighbouring houses,—this alley, it seems, being noted for the profligacy of its inhabitants.

When I reflected that a wretched hovel like this had been, probably, the last retreat of the Dudleys, when I painted their sufferings, of which the numberless tales of distress of which I had lately been an auditor enabled me to form an adequate conception, I felt as if to lie down and expire on the very spot where Constantia had fallen was the only sacrifice to friendship which time had left to me.

From this house I wandered to the field where the dead had been, promiscuously and by hundreds, interred. I counted the long series of graves, which were closely ranged, and, being recently levelled, exhibited the appearance of a harrowed field. Methought I could have given thousands to know in what spot the body of my friend lay, that I might moisten the sacred earth with my tears. Boards hastily nailed together formed the best receptacle which the exigencies of the time could grant to the dead. Many corpses were thrown into a single excavation, and all distinctions founded on merit and rank were obliterated. The father and child had been placed in the same cart and thrown into the same hole.

Despairing, by any longer stay in the city, to effect my purpose, and the period of my embarkation being near, I prepared to resume my journey. I should have set out the next day, but, a family with whom I had made acquaintance expecting to proceed to New York within a week, I consented to be their companion, and, for that end, to delay my departure.

Meanwhile, I shut myself up in my apartment, and pursued avocations that were adapted to the melancholy tenor of my thoughts. The day preceding that appointed for my journey arrived. It was necessary to complete my arrangements with the family with whom I was to travel, and to settle with the lady whose apartments I occupied.

On how slender threads does our destiny hang! Had not a momentary impulse tempted me to sing my favourite ditty to the harpsichord, to beguile the short interval during which my hostess was conversing with her visitor in the next apartment, I should have speeded to New York, have embarked for Europe, and been eternally severed from my friend, whom I believed to have died in frenzy and beggary, but who was alive and affluent, and who sought me with a diligence scarcely inferior to my own. We imagined ourselves severed from each other by death or by impassable seas; but, at the moment when our hopes had sunk to the lowest ebb, a mysterious destiny conducted our footsteps to the same spot.

I heard a murmuring exclamation; I heard my hostess call, in a voice of terror, for help; I rushed into the room; I saw one stretched on the floor, in the attitude of death; I sprung forward and fixed my eyes upon her countenance; I clasped my hands and articulated, "Constantia!"

She speedily recovered from her swoon. Her eyes opened; she moved, she spoke. Still methought it was an illusion of the senses that created the phantom. I could not bear to withdraw my eyes from her countenance. If they wandered for a moment, I fell into doubt and perplexity, and again fixed them upon her, to assure myself of her existence.

The succeeding three days were spent in a state of dizziness and intoxication. The ordinary functions of nature were disturbed. The appetite for sleep and for food were confounded and lost amidst the impetuosities of a master-passion. To look and to talk to each other afforded enchanting occupation for every moment. I would not part from her side, but eat and slept, walked and mused and read, with my arm locked in hers, and with her breath fanning my cheek.

I have indeed much to learn. Sophia Courtland has never been wise. Her affections disdain the cold dictates of discretion, and spurn at every limit that contending duties and mixed obligations prescribe.

And yet, O precious inebriation of the heart! O pre-eminent love! what pleasure of reason or of sense can stand in competition with those attendant upon thee? Whether thou hiest to the fanes of a benevolent deity, or layest all thy homage at the feet of one who most visibly resembles the perfections of our Maker, surely thy sanction is divine, thy boon is happiness!

CHAPTER VII.

The tumults of curiosity and pleasure did not speedily subside. The story of each other's wanderings was told with endless amplification and minuteness. Henceforth, the stream of our existence was to mix; we were to act and to think in common; casual witnesses and written testimony should become superfluous. Eyes and ears were to be eternally employed upon the conduct of each other; death, when it should come, was not to be deplored, because it was an unavoidable and brief privation to her that should survive. Being, under any modification, is dear; but that state to which death is a passage is all-desirable to virtue and all-compensating to grief.

Meanwhile, precedent events were made the themes of endless conversation. Every incident and passion in the course of four years was revived and exhibited. The name of Ormond was, of course, frequently repeated by my friend. His features and deportment were described; her meditations and resolutions, with regard to him, fully disclosed. My counsel was asked, in what manner it became her to act.

I could not but harbour aversion to a scheme which should tend to sever me from Constantia, or to give me a competitor in her affections. Besides this, the properties of Ormond were of too mysterious a nature to make him worthy of acceptance. Little more was known concerning him than what he himself had disclosed to the Dudleys, but this knowledge would suffice to invalidate his claims.

He had dwelt, in his conversations with Constantia, sparingly on his own concerns. Yet he did not hide from her that he had been left in early youth to his own guidance; that he had embraced, when almost a child, the trade of arms; that he had found service and promotion in the armies of Potemkin and Romanzow; that he had executed secret and diplomatic functions at Constantinople and Berlin; that in the latter city he had met with schemers and reasoners who aimed at the new-modelling of the world, and the subversion of all that has hitherto been conceived elementary and fundamental in the constitution of man and of government; that some of those reformers had secretly united to break down the military and monarchical fabric of German policy; that others, more wisely, had devoted their secret efforts, not to overturn, but to build; that, for this end, they embraced an exploring and colonizing project; that he had allied himself to these, and for the promotion of their projects had spent six years of his life in journeys by sea and land, in tracts unfrequented till then by any European.

What were the moral or political maxims which this adventurous and visionary sect had adopted, and what was the seat of their new-born empire, —whether on the shore of an *austral* continent, or in the heart of desert America,—he carefully concealed. These were exhibited or hidden, or shifted, according to his purpose. Not to reveal too much, and not to tire curiosity or overtask belief, was his daily labour. He talked of alliance with the family whose name he bore, and who had lost their honours and estates by the Hanoverian succession to the crown of England.

I had seen too much of innovation and imposture, in, France and Italy, not to regard a man like this with aversion and fear. The mind of my friend was wavering and unsuspicious. She had lived at a distance from scenes where principles are hourly put to the test of experiment; where all extremes of fortitude and pusillanimity are accustomed to meet; where recluse virtue and speculative heroism gives place, as if by magic, to the last excesses of debauchery and wickedness; where pillage and murder are engrafted on systems of all-embracing and self-oblivious benevolence, and the good of mankind is professed to be pursued with bonds of association and covenants of secrecy. Hence, my friend had decided without the sanction of experience, had allowed herself to wander into untried paths, and had hearkened to positions pregnant with destruction and ignominy.

It was not difficult to exhibit in their true light the enormous errors of this man, and the danger of prolonging their intercourse. Her assent to accompany me to England was readily obtained. Too much despatch could not be used; but the disposal of her property must first take place. This was necessarily productive of some delay.

I had been made, contrary to inclination, expert in the management of all affairs relative to property. My mother's lunacy, subsequent disease, and death, had imposed upon me obligations and cares little suitable to my sex and age. They could not be eluded or transferred to others; and, by degrees, experience enlarged my knowledge and familiarized my tasks.

It was agreed that I should visit and inspect my friend's estate in Jersey, while she remained in her present abode, to put an end to the views and expectations of Ormond, and to make preparation for her voyage. We were reconciled to a temporary separation by the necessity that prescribed it.

During our residence together, the mind of Constantia was kept in perpetual ferment. The second day after my departure, the turbulence of her feelings began to subside, and she found herself at leisure to pursue those measures which her present situation prescribed.

The time prefixed by Ormond for the termination of his absence had nearly arrived. Her resolutions respecting this man, lately formed, now occurred to her. Her heart drooped as she revolved the necessity of disuniting their fates; but that this disunion was proper could not admit of doubt. How information of her present views might be most satisfactorily imparted to him, was a question not instantly decided. She reflected on the impetuosity of his character, and conceived that her intentions might be most conveniently unfolded in a letter. This letter she immediately sat down to write. Just then the door opened, and Ormond entered the apartment.

She was somewhat, and for a moment, startled by this abrupt and unlooked-for entrance. Yet she greeted him with pleasure. Her greeting was received with coldness. A second glance at his countenance informed her that his mind was somewhat discomposed.

Folding his hands on his breast, ho stalked to the window and looked up at the moon. Presently he withdrew his gaze from this object, and fixed it upon Constantia. He spoke, but his words were produced by a kind of effort.

"Fit emblem," he exclaimed, "of human versatility! One impediment is gone. I hoped it was the only one. But no! the removal of that merely made room for another. Let this be removed. Well, fate will interplace a third. All our toils will thus be frustrated, and the ruin will finally redound upon our heads." There he stopped.

This strain could not be interpreted by Constantia. She smiled, and, without noticing his incoherences, proceeded to inquire into his adventures during their separation. He listened to her, but his eyes, fixed upon hers, and his solemnity of aspect, were immovable. When she paused, he seated himself close to her, and, grasping her hand with a vehemence that almost pained her, said,—

"Look at me; steadfastly. Can you read my thoughts? Can your discernment reach the bounds of my knowledge and the bottom of my purposes? Catch you not a view of the monsters that are starting into birth *here*?" (and he put his left hand to his forehead.) "But you cannot. Should I paint them to you verbally, you would call me jester or deceiver. What pity that you have not instruments for piercing into thoughts!"

"I presume," said Constantia, affecting cheerfulness which she did not feel, "such instruments would be useless to me. You never scruple to say what you think. Your designs are no sooner conceived than they are expressed. All you know, all you wish, and all you purpose, are known to others as soon as to yourself. No scruples of decorum, no foresight of consequences, are obstacles in your way."

"True," replied he; "all obstacles are trampled under foot but one."

"What is the insuperable one?"

"Incredulity in him that hears. I must not say what will not be credited. I must not relate feats and avow schemes, when my hearer will say, 'Those feats were never performed; these schemes are not yours.' I care not if the truth of my tenets and the practicability of my purposes be denied. Still, I will openly maintain them; but when my assertions will themselves be disbelieved, when it is denied that I adopt the creed and project the plans which I affirm to be adopted and projected by me, it is needless to affirm.

"To-morrow I mean to ascertain the height of the lunar mountains by travelling to the top of them. Then I will station myself in the track of the last comet, and wait till its circumvolution suffers me to leap upon it; then, by walking on its surface, I will ascertain whether it be hot enough to burn my soles. Do you believe that this can be done?"

"No."

"Do you believe, in consequence of my assertion, that I design to do this, and that, in my apprehension, it is easy to be done?"

"Not unless I previously believe you to be lunatic."

"Then why should I assert my purposes? Why speak, when the hearer will infer nothing from my speech but that I am either lunatic or liar?"

"In that predicament, silence is best."

"In that predicament I now stand. I am not going to unfold myself. Just now, I pitied thee for want of eyes. 'Twas a foolish compassion. Thou art happy, because thou seest not an inch before thee or behind." Here he was for a moment buried in thought; then, breaking from his reverie, he said, "So your father is dead?"

"True," said Constantia, endeavouring to suppress her rising emotions; "he is no more. It is so recent an event that I imagined you a stranger to it."

"False imagination! Thinkest thou I would refrain from knowing what so nearly concerns us both? Perhaps your opinion of my ignorance extends beyond this. Perhaps I know not your fruitless search for a picture. Perhaps I neither followed you nor led you to a being called Sophia Courtland. I was not present at the meeting. I am unapprized of the effects of your romantic passion for each other. I did not witness the rapturous effusions and inexorable counsels of the newcomer. I know not the contents of the letter which you are preparing to write."

As he spoke this, the accents of Ormond gradually augmented in vehemence. His countenance bespoke a deepening inquietude and growing passion. He stopped at the mention of the letter, because his voice was overpowered by emotion. This pause afforded room for the astonishment of Constantia. Her interviews and conversations with me took place at seasons of general repose, when all doors were fast and avenues shut, in the midst of silence, and in the bosom of retirement. The theme of our discourse was, commonly, too sacred for any ears but our own; disclosures were of too intimate and delicate a nature for any but a female audience; they were too injurious to the fame and peace of Ormond for him to be admitted to partake of them: yet his words implied a full acquaintance with recent events, and with purposes and deliberations shrouded, as we imagined, in impenetrable secrecy.

As soon as Constantia recovered from the confusion of these thoughts, she eagerly questioned him:—"What do you know? How do you know what has happened, or what is intended?"

"Poor Constantia!" he exclaimed, in a tone bitter and sarcastic. "How hopeless is thy ignorance! To enlighten thee is past my power. What do I know? Every thing. Not a tittle has escaped me. Thy letter is superfluous; I know its contents before they are written. I was to be told that a soldier and a traveller, a man who refused his faith to dreams, and his homage to shadows, merited only scorn and forgetfulness. That thy affections and person were due to another; that intercourse between us was henceforth to cease; that preparation was making for a voyage to Britain, and that Ormond was to walk to his grave alone!"

In spite of harsh tones and inflexible features, these words were accompanied with somewhat that betrayed a mind full of discord and agony. Constantia's astonishment was mingled with dejection. The discovery of a passion deeper and less curable than she suspected—the perception of embarrassments and difficulties in the path which she had chosen, that had not previously occurred to her—threw her mind into anxious suspense.

The measures she had previously concerted were still approved. To part from Ormond was enjoined by every dictate of discretion and duty. An explanation of her motives and views could not take place more seasonably than at present. Every consideration of justice to herself and humanity to Ormond made it desirable that this interview should be the last. By inexplicable means, he had gained a knowledge of her intentions. It was expedient, therefore, to state them with clearness and force. In what words this was to be done, was the subject of momentary deliberation.

Her thoughts were discerned, and her speech anticipated, by her companion:
—"Why droopest thou, and why thus silent, Constantia? The secret of thy fate will never be detected. Till thy destiny be finished, it will not be the topic of a single fear. But not for thyself, but me, art thou concerned. Thou dreadest, yet determinest, to confirm my predictions of thy voyage to Europe and thy severance from me.

"Dismiss thy inquietudes on that score. What misery thy scorn and thy rejection are able to inflict is inflicted already. Thy decision was known to me as soon as it was formed. Thy motives were known. Not an argument or plea of thy counsellor, not a syllable of her invective, not a sound of her persuasive rhetoric, escaped my hearing. I know thy decree to be immutable. As my doubts, so my wishes have taken their flight. Perhaps, in the depth of thy ignorance, it was supposed that I should struggle to reverse thy purpose by menaces or supplications; that I should boast of the cruelty with which I should avenge an imaginary wrong upon myself. No. All is very well. Go. Not a whisper of objection or reluctance shalt thou hear from me."

"If I could think," said Constantia, with tremulous hesitation, "that you part from me without anger; that you see the rectitude of my proceeding—"

"Anger! Rectitude! I pr'ythee, peace. I know thou art going.—I know that all objection to thy purpose would be vain. Thinkest thou that thy stay, undictated by love, the mere fruit of compassion, would afford me pleasure or crown my wishes? No. I am not so dastardly a wretch. There was something in thy power to bestow, but thy will accords not with thy power. I merit not the boon, and thou refusest it. I am content."

Here Ormond fixed more significant eyes upon her. "Poor Constantia!" he continued. "Shall I warn thee of the danger that awaits thee? For what end? To elude it is impossible. It will come, and thou, perhaps, wilt be unhappy. Foresight that enables not to shun, only precreates, the evil.

"Come it will. Though future, it knows not the empire of contingency. An inexorable and immutable decree enjoins it. Perhaps it is thy nature to meet with calmness what cannot be shunned. Perhaps, when it is past, thy reason will perceive its irrevocable nature, and restore thee to peace. Such is the conduct of the wise; but such, I fear, the education of Constantia Dudley will debar her from pursuing.

"Fain would I regard it as the test of thy wisdom. I look upon thy past life. All the forms of genuine adversity have beset thy youth. Poverty, disease, servile labour, a criminal and hapless parent, have been evils which thou hast not ungracefully sustained. An absent friend and murdered father were added to thy list of woes, and here thy courage was deficient. Thy soul was proof against substantial misery, but sunk into helpless cowardice at the sight of phantoms.

"One more disaster remains. To call it by its true name would be useless or pernicious. Useless, because thou wouldst pronounce its occurrence impossible; pernicious, because, if its possibility were granted, the omen would distract thee with fear. How shall I describe it? Is it loss of fame? No. The deed will be unwitnessed by a human creature. Thy reputation will be spotless, for nothing will be done by thee unsuitable to the tenor of thy past life. Calumny will not be heard to whisper. All that know thee will be lavish of their eulogies as ever. Their eulogies will be as justly merited. Of this merit thou wilt entertain as just and as adequate conceptions as now.

"It is no repetition of the evils thou hast already endured; it is neither drudgery, nor sickness, nor privation of friends. Strange perverseness of human reason! It is an evil; it will be thought upon with agony; it will close up all the sources of pleasurable recollection; it will exterminate hope; it will endear oblivion, and push thee into an untimely grave. Yet to grasp it is impossible. The moment we inspect it nearly, it vanishes. Thy claims to human approbation and divine applause will be undiminished and unaltered by it. The testimony of approving conscience will have lost none of its explicitness and energy. Yet thou wilt feed upon sighs; thy tears will flow without remission; thou wilt grow enamoured of death, and perhaps wilt anticipate the stroke of disease.

"Yet perhaps my prediction is groundless as my knowledge. Perhaps thy discernment will avail to make thee wise and happy. Perhaps thou wilt perceive thy privilege of sympathetic and intellectual activity to be untouched. Heaven grant the non-fulfilment of my prophecy, thy disenthralment from error, and the perpetuation of thy happiness."

Saying this, Ormond withdrew. His words were always accompanied with gestures and looks and tones that fastened the attention of the hearer; but the terms of his present discourse afforded, independently of gesticulation and utterance, sufficient motives to attention and remembrance. He was gone, but his image was contemplated by Constantia; his words still rung in her ears.

The letter she designed to compose was rendered, by this interview, unnecessary. Meanings of which she and her friend alone were conscious were discovered by Ormond, through some other medium than words; yet that was impossible. A being unendowed with preternatural attributes could gain the information which this man possessed, only by the exertion of his senses.

All human precautions had been used to baffle the attempts of any secret witness. She recalled to mind the circumstances in which conversations with her friend had taken place. All had been retirement, secrecy, and silence. The hours usually dedicated to sleep had been devoted to this better purpose. Much had been said, in a voice low and scarcely louder than a whisper. To have overheard it at the distance of a few feet was apparently impossible.

Their conversations had not been recorded by her. It could not be believed that this had been done by Sophia Courtland. Had Ormond and her friend met during the interval that had elapsed between her separation from the latter and her meeting with the former? Human events are conjoined by links imperceptible to keenest eyes. Of Ormond's means of information she was wholly unapprized. Perhaps accident would some time unfold them. One thing was incontestable:—that her schemes and her reasons for adopting them were known to him.

What unforeseen effects had that knowledge produced! In what ambiguous terms had he couched his prognostics of some mighty evil that awaited her! He had given a terrible but contradictory description of her destiny. An event was to happen, akin to no calamity which she had already endured, disconnected with all which the imagination of man is accustomed to deprecate, capable of urging her to suicide, and yet of a kind which left it undecided whether she would regard it with indifference.

49

What reliance should she place upon prophetic incoherences thus wild? What precautions should she take against a danger thus inscrutable and imminent?

CHAPTER VIII.

These incidents and reflections were speedily transmitted to me. I had always believed the character and machinations of Ormond to be worthy of caution and fear. His means of information I did not pretend, and thought it useless, to investigate. We cannot hide our actions and thoughts from one of powerful sagacity, whom the detection sufficiently interests to make him use all the methods of detection in his power. The study of concealment is, in all cases, fruitless or hurtful. All that duty enjoins is to design and to execute nothing which may not be approved by a divine and omniscient Observer. Human scrutiny is neither to be solicited nor shunned. Human approbation or censure can never be exempt from injustice, because our limited perceptions debar us from a thorough knowledge of any actions and motives but our own.

On reviewing what had passed between Constantia and me, I recollected nothing incompatible with purity and rectitude. That Ormond was apprized of all that had passed, I by no means inferred from the tenor of his conversation with Constantia; nor, if this had been incontestably proved, should I have experienced any trepidation or anxiety on that account.

His obscure and indirect menaces of evil were of more importance. His discourse on this topic seemed susceptible only of two constructions. Either he intended some fatal mischief, and was willing to torment her by fears, while he concealed from her the nature of her danger, that he might hinder her from guarding her safety by suitable precautions; or, being hopeless of rendering her propitious to his wishes, his malice was satisfied with leaving her a legacy of apprehension and doubt. Constantia's unacquaintance with the doctrines of that school in which Ormond was probably instructed led her to regard the conduct of this man with more curiosity and wonder than fear. She saw nothing but a disposition to sport with her ignorance and bewilder her with doubts.

I do not believe myself destitute of courage. Rightly to estimate the danger and encounter it with firmness are worthy of a rational being; but to place our security in thoughtlessness and blindness is only less ignoble than cowardice. I could not forget the proofs of violence which accompanied the death of Mr. Dudley. I could not overlook, in the recent conversation with Constantia, Ormond's allusion to her murdered father. It was possible that the nature of this death had been accidentally imparted to him; but it was likewise possible that his was the knowledge of one who performed the act.

The enormity of this deed appeared by no means incongruous with the sentiments of Ormond. Human life is momentous or trivial in our eyes, according to the course which our habits and opinions have taken. Passion greedily accepts, and habit readily offers, the sacrifice of another's life, and reason obeys the impulse of education and desire.

A youth of eighteen, a volunteer in a Russian army encamped in Bessarabia, made prey of a Tartar girl, found in the field of a recent battle. Conducting her to his quarters, he met a friend, who, on some pretence, claimed the victim. From angry words they betook themselves to swords. A combat ensued, in which the first claimant ran his antagonist through the body. He then bore his prize unmolested away, and, having exercised brutality of one kind upon the helpless victim, stabbed her to the heart, as an offering to the *manes* of Sarsefield, the friend whom he had slain. Next morning, willing more signally to expiate his guilt, he rushed alone upon a troop of Turkish foragers, and brought away five heads, suspended, by their gory locks, to his horse's mane. These he cast upon the grave of Sarsefield, and conceived himself fully to have expiated yesterday's offence. In reward for his prowess, the general gave him a commission in the Cossack troops. This youth was Ormond; and such is a specimen of his exploits during a military career of eight years, in a warfare the most savage and implacable, and, at the same time, the most iniquitous and wanton, which history records.

With passions and habits like these, the life of another was a trifling sacrifice to vengeance or impatience. How Mr. Dudley had excited the resentment of Ormond, by what means the assassin had accomplished his intention without awakening alarm or incurring suspicion, it was not for me to discover. The inextricability of human events, the imperviousness of cunning, and the obduracy of malice, I had frequent occasions to remark.

I did not labour to vanquish the security of my friend. As to precautions, they were useless. There was no fortress, guarded by barriers of stone and iron and watched by sentinels that never slept, to which she might retire from his stratagems. If there were such a retreat, it would scarcely avail her against a foe circumspect and subtle as Ormond.

I pondered on the condition of my friend. I reviewed the incidents of her life. I compared her lot with that of others. I could not but discover a sort of incurable malignity in her fate. I felt as if it were denied to her to enjoy a long life or permanent tranquillity. I asked myself what she had done, entitling her to this incessant persecution. Impatience and murmuring took place of sorrow and fear in my heart. When I reflected that all human agency was merely subservient to a divine purpose, I fell into fits of accusation and impiety.

This injustice was transient, and soberer views convinced me that every scheme, comprising the whole, must be productive of partial and temporary evil. The sufferings of Constantia were limited to a moment; they were the unavoidable appendages of terrestrial existence; they formed the only avenue to wisdom, and the only claim to uninterrupted fruition and eternal repose in an after-scene.

The course of my reflections, and the issue to which they led, were unforeseen by myself. Fondly as I doted upon this woman, methought I could resign her to the grave without a murmur or a tear. While my thoughts were calmed by resignation, and my fancy occupied with nothing but the briefness of that space and evanescence of that time which severs the living from the dead, I contemplated, almost with complacency, a violent or untimely close to her existence.

This loftiness of mind could not always be accomplished or constantly maintained. One effect of my fears was to hasten my departure to Europe. There existed no impediment but the want of a suitable conveyance. In the first packet that should leave America, it was determined to secure a passage. Mr. Melbourne consented to take charge of Constantia's property, and, after the sale of it, to transmit to her the money that should thence arise.

Meanwhile, I was anxious that Constantia should leave her present abode and join me in New York. She willingly adopted this arrangement, but conceived it necessary to spend a few days at her house in Jersey. She could reach the latter place without much deviation from the straight road, and she was desirous of resurveying a spot where many of her infantile days had been spent.

This house and domain I have already mentioned to have once belonged to Mr. Dudley. It was selected with the judgement and adorned with the taste of a disciple of the schools of Florence and Vicenza. In his view, cultivation was subservient to the picturesque, and a mansion was erected, eminent for nothing but chastity of ornaments and simplicity of structure. The massive parts were of stone; the outer surfaces were smooth, snow-white, and diversified by apertures and cornices, in which a cement uncommonly tenacious was wrought into proportions the most correct and forms the most graceful. The floors, walls, and ceilings, consisted of a still more exquisitely-tempered substance, and were painted by Mr. Dudley's own hand. All appendages of this building, as seats, tables, and cabinets, were modelled by the owner's particular direction, and in a manner scrupulously classical.

He had scarcely entered on the enjoyment of this splendid possession, when it was ravished away. No privation was endured with more impatience than this; but, happily, it was purchased by one who left Mr. Dudley's arrangements unmolested, and who shortly after conveyed it entire to Ormond. By him it was finally appropriated to the use of Helena Cleves, and now, by a singular contexture of events, it had reverted to those hands in which the death of the original proprietor, if no other change had been made in his condition, would have left it. The farm still remained in the tenure of a German emigrant, who held it partly on condition of preserving the garden and mansion in safety and in perfect order.

This retreat was now revisited by Constantia, after an interval of four years. Autumn had made some progress, but the aspect of nature was, so to speak, more significant than at any other season. She was agreeably accommodated under the tenant's roof, and found a nameless pleasure in traversing spaces in which every object prompted an endless train of recollections.

Her sensations were not foreseen. They led to a state of mind inconsistent, in some degree, with the projects adopted in obedience to the suggestions of a friend. Every thing in this scene had been created and modelled by the genius of her father. It was a kind of fane, sanctified by his imaginary presence.

To consign the fruits of his industry and invention to foreign and unsparing hands seemed a kind of sacrilege, for which she almost feared that the dead would rise to upbraid her. Those images which bind us to our natal soil, to the abode of our innocent and careless youth, were recalled to her fancy by the scenes which she now beheld. These were enforced by considerations of the dangers which attended her voyage from storms and from enemies, and from the tendency to revolution and war which seemed to actuate all the nations of Europe. Her native country was by no means exempt from similar tendencies, but these evils were less imminent, and its manners and government, in their present modifications, were unspeakably more favourable to the dignity and improvement of the human race than those which prevailed in any part of the ancient world.

My solicitations and my obligation to repair to England overweighed her objections, but her new reflections led her to form new determinations with regard to this part of her property. She concluded to retain possession, and hoped that some future event would allow her to return to this favourite spot without forfeiture of my society. An abode of some years in Europe would more eminently qualify her for the enjoyment of retirement and safety in her native country. The time that should elapse before her embarkation, she was desirous of passing among the shades of this romantic retreat.

I was by no means reconciled to this proceeding. I loved my friend too well to endure any needless separation without repining. In addition to this, the image of Ormond haunted my thoughts, and gave birth to incessant but indefinable fears. I believed that her safety would very little depend upon the nature of her abode, or the number or watchfulness of her companions. My nearness to her person would frustrate no stratagem, nor promote any other end than my own entanglement in the same fold. Still, that I was not apprized each hour of her condition, that her state was lonely and sequestered, were sources of disquiet, the obvious remedy to which was her coming to New York. Preparations for departure were assigned to me, and these required my continuance in the city.

Once a week, Laffert, her tenant, visited, for purposes of traffic, the city. He was the medium of our correspondence. To him I intrusted a letter, in which my dissatisfaction at her absence, and the causes which gave it birth, were freely confessed.

The confidence of safety seldom deserted my friend. Since her mysterious conversation with Ormond, he had utterly vanished. Previous to that interview, his visits or his letters were incessant and punctual; but since, no token was given that he existed. Two months had elapsed. He gave her no reason to expect a cessation of intercourse. He had parted from her with his usual abruptness and informality. She did not conceive it incumbent on her to search him out, but she would not have been displeased with an opportunity to discuss with him more fully the motives of her conduct. This opportunity had been hitherto denied.

Her occupations in her present retreat were, for the most part, dictated by caprice or by chance. The mildness of autumn permitted her to ramble, during the day, from one rock and one grove to another. There was a luxury in musing, and in the sensations which the scenery and silence produced, which, in consequence of her long estrangement from them, were accompanied with all the attractions of novelty, and from which she would not consent to withdraw.

In the evening she usually retired to the mansion, and shut herself up in that apartment which, in the original structure of the house, had been designed for study, and no part of whose furniture had been removed or displaced. It was a kind of closet on the second floor, illuminated by a spacious window, through which a landscape of uncommon amplitude and beauty was presented to the view. Here the pleasures of the day were revived, by recalling and enumerating them in letters to her friend. She always quitted this recess with reluctance, and seldom till the night was half spent.

One evening she retired hither when the sun had just dipped beneath the horizon. Her implements of writing were prepared; but, before the pen was assumed, her eyes rested for a moment on the variegated hues which were poured out upon the western sky and upon the scene of intermingled waters, copses, and fields. The view comprised a part of the road which led to this dwelling. It was partially and distantly seen, and the passage of horses or men was betokened chiefly by the dust which was raised by their footsteps.

A token of this kind now caught her attention. It fixed her eye chiefly by the picturesque effect produced by interposing its obscurity between her and the splendours which the sun had left. Presently she gained a faint view of a man and horse. This circumstance laid no claim to attention, and she was withdrawing her eye, when the traveller's stopping and dismounting at the gate made her renew her scrutiny. This was reinforced by something in the figure and movements of the horseman which reminded her of Ormond.

She started from her seat with some degree of palpitation. Whence this arose, whether from fear or from joy, or from intermixed emotions, it would not be easy to ascertain. Having entered the gate, the visitant, remounting his horse, set the animal on full speed. Every moment brought him nearer, and added to her first belief. He stopped not till he reached the mansion. The person of Ormond was distinctly recognised.

An interview at this dusky and lonely hour, in circumstances so abrupt and unexpected, could not fail to surprise, and, in some degree, to alarm. The substance of his last conversation was recalled. The evils which were darkly and ambiguously predicted thronged to her memory. It seemed as if the present moment was to be, in some way, decisive of her fate. This visit she did not hesitate to suppose designed for her, but somewhat uncommonly momentous must have prompted him to take so long a journey.

The rooms on the lower floor were dark, the windows and doors being fastened. She had entered the house by the principal door, and this was the only one at present unlocked. The room in which she sat was over the hall, and the massive door beneath could not be opened without noisy signals. The question that occurred to her, by what means Ormond would gain admittance to her presence, she supposed would be instantly decided. She listened to hear his footsteps on the pavement, or the creaking of hinges. The silence, however, continued profound as before.

After a minute's pause, she approached the window more nearly and endeavoured to gain a view of the space before the house. She saw nothing but the horse, whose bridle was thrown over his neck, and who was left at liberty to pick up what scanty herbage the lawn afforded to his hunger. The rider had disappeared.

It now occurred to her that this visit had a purpose different from that which she at first conjectured. It was easily conceived that Ormond was unacquainted with her residence at this spot. The knowledge could only be imparted to him by indirect or illicit means. That these means had been employed by him, she was by no means authorized to infer from the silence and distance he had lately maintained. But if an interview with her were not the purpose of his coming, how should she interpret it?

CHAPTER IX.

While occupied with these reflections, the light hastily disappeared, and darkness, rendered, by a cloudy atmosphere, uncommonly intense, succeeded. She had the means of lighting a lamp that hung against the wall, but had been too much immersed in thought to notice the deepening of the gloom. Recovering from her reverie, she looked around her with some degree of trepidation, and prepared to strike a spark that would enable her to light her lamp.

She had hitherto indulged an habitual indifference to danger. Now the presence of Ormond, the unknown purpose that led him hither, and the defencelessness of her condition, inspired her with apprehensions to which she had hitherto been a stranger. She had been accustomed to pass many nocturnal hours in this closet. Till now, nothing had occurred that made her enter it with circumspection or continue in it with reluctance.

Her sensations were no longer tranquil. Each minute that she spent in this recess appeared to multiply her hazards. To linger here appeared to her the height of culpable temerity. She hastily resolved to return to the farmer's dwelling, and, on the morrow, to repair to New York. For this end she was desirous to produce a light. The materials were at hand.

She lifted her hand to strike the flint, when her ear caught a sound which betokened the opening of the door that led into the next apartment. Her motion was suspended, and she listened as well as a throbbing heart would permit. That Ormond's was the hand that opened, was the first suggestion of her fears. The motives of this unseasonable entrance could not be reconciled with her safety. He had given no warning of his approach, and the door was opened with tardiness and seeming caution.

Sounds continued, of which no distinct conception could be obtained, or the cause that produced them assigned. The floors of every apartment being composed, like the walls and ceiling, of cement, footsteps were rendered almost undistinguishable. It was plain, however, that some one approached her own door.

The panic and confusion that now invaded her was owing to surprise, and to the singularity of her situation. The mansion was desolate and lonely. It was night. She was immersed in darkness. She had not the means, and was unaccustomed to the office, of repelling personal injuries. What injuries she had reason to dread, who was the agent, and what were his motives, were subjects Of vague and incoherent meditation.

Meanwhile, low and imperfect sounds, that had in them more of inanimate than human, assailed her ear. Presently they ceased. An inexplicable fear deterred her from calling. Light would have exercised a friendly influence. This it was in her power to produce, but not without motion and noise; and these, by occasioning the discovery of her being in the closet, might possibly enhance her danger.

Conceptions like these were unworthy of the mind of Constantia. An interval of silence succeeded, interrupted only by the whistling of the blast without. It was sufficient for the restoration of her courage. She blushed at the cowardice which had trembled at a sound. She considered that Ormond might, indeed, be near, but that he was probably unconscious of her situation. His coming was not with the circumspection of an enemy. He might be acquainted with the place of her retreat, and had come to obtain an interview, with no clandestine or mysterious purposes. The noises she had heard had, doubtless, proceeded from the next apartment, but might be produced by some harmless or vagrant creature.

These considerations restored her tranquillity. They enabled her, deliberately, to create a light, but they did not dissuade her from leaving the house. Omens of evil seemed to be connected with this solitary and darksome abode. Besides, Ormond had unquestionably entered upon this scene It could not be doubted that she was the object of his visit. The farm-house was a place of meeting more suitable and safe than any other. Thither, therefore, she determined immediately to return.

The closet had but one door, and this led into the chamber where the sounds had arisen. Through this chamber, therefore, she was obliged to pass, in order to reach the staircase, which terminated in the hall below.

Bearing the light in her left hand, she withdrew the bolt of the door and opened. In spite of courageous efforts, she opened with unwillingness, and shuddered to throw a glance forward or advance a step into the room. This was not needed, to reveal to her the cause of her late disturbance. Her eye instantly lighted on the body of a man, supine, motionless, stretched on the floor, close to the door through which she was about to pass.

A spectacle like this was qualified to startle her. She shrunk back, and fixed a more steadfast eye upon the prostrate person. There was no mark of blood or of wounds, but there was something in the attitude more significant of death than of sleep. His face rested on the floor, and his ragged locks concealed what part of his visage was not hidden by his posture. His garb was characterized by fashionable elegance, but was polluted with dust.

The image that first occurred to her was that of Ormond. This instantly gave place to another, which was familiar to her apprehension. It was at first too indistinctly seen to suggest a name. She continued to gaze and to be lost in fearful astonishment. Was this the person whose entrance had been overheard, and who had dragged himself hither to die at her door? Yet, in that case, would not groans and expiring efforts have testified his condition and invoked her succour? Was he not brought hither in the arms of his assassin? She mused upon the possible motives that induced some one thus to act, and upon the connection that might subsist between her destiny and that of the dead.

Her meditations, however fruitless in other respects, could not fail to show her the propriety of hastening from this spot. To scrutinize the form or face of the dead was a task to which her courage was unequal. Suitably accompanied and guarded, she would not scruple to return and ascertain, by the most sedulous examination, the cause of this ominous event.

She stepped over the breathless corpse, and hurried to the staircase. It became her to maintain the command of her muscles and joints, and to proceed without faltering or hesitation. Scarcely had she reached the entrance of the hall, when, casting anxious looks forward, she beheld a human figure. No scrutiny was requisite to inform her that this was Ormond.

She stopped. He approached her with looks and gestures placid but solemn. There was nothing in his countenance rugged or malignant. On the contrary, there were tokens of compassion.

"So," said he, "I expected to meet you. Alight, gleaming from the window, marked you out. This and Laffert's directions have guided me."

"What," said Constantia, with discomposure in her accent, "was your motive for seeking me?"

"Have you forgotten," said Ormond, "what passed at our last interview? The evil that I then predicted is at hand. Perhaps you were incredulous; you accounted me a madman or deceiver; now I am come to witness the fulfilment of my words and the completion of your destiny. To rescue you I have not come: that is not within the compass of human powers.

"Poor Constantia," he continued, in tones that manifested genuine sympathy, "look upon thyself as lost. The toils that beset thee are inextricable. Summon up thy patience to endure the evil. Now will the last and heaviest trial betide thy fortitude. I could weep for thee, if my manly nature would permit. This is the scene of thy calamity, and this the hour."

These words were adapted to excite curiosity mingled with terror. Ormond's deportment was of an unexampled tenor, as well as that evil which he had so ambiguously predicted. He offered no protection from danger, and yet gave no proof of being himself an agent or auxiliary. After a minute's pause, Constantia, recovering a firm tone, said,—

"Mr. Ormond, your recent deportment but ill accords with your professions of sincerity and plain dealing. What your purpose is, or whether you have any purpose, I am at a loss to conjecture. Whether you most deserve censure or ridicule, is a point which you afford me not the means of deciding, and to which, unless on your own account, I am indifferent. If you are willing to be more explicit, or if there be any topic on which you wish further to converse, I will not refuse your company to Laffert's dwelling. Longer to remain here would be indiscreet and absurd."

So saying, she motioned towards the door. Ormond was passive, and seemed indisposed to prevent her departure, till she laid her hand upon the lock. He then, without moving from his place, exclaimed,—

"Stay! Must this meeting, which fate ordains to be the last, be so short? Must a time and place so suitable for what remains to be said and done be neglected or misused? No. You charge me with duplicity, and deem my conduct either ridiculous or criminal. I have stated my reasons for concealment, but these have failed to convince you. Well, here is now an end to doubt. All ambiguities are preparing to vanish."

When Ormond began to speak, Constantia paused to hearken to him. His vehemence was not of that nature which threatened to obstruct her passage. It was by entreaty that he apparently endeavoured to detain her steps, and not by violence. Hence arose her patience to listen. He continued:—

"Constantia! thy father is dead. Art thou not desirous of detecting the author of his fate? Will it afford thee no consolation to know that the deed is punished? Wilt thou suffer me to drag the murderer to thy feet? Thy justice will be gratified by this sacrifice. Somewhat will be due to him who avenged thy wrong in the blood of the perpetrator. What sayest thou? Grant me thy permission, and in a moment I will drag him hither."

These words called up the image of the person whose corpse she had lately seen. It was readily conceived that to him Ormond alluded; but this was the assassin of her father, and his crime had been detected and punished by Ormond! These images had no other effect than to urge her departure: she again applied her hand to the lock, and said,—

"This scene must not be prolonged. My father's death I desire not to hear explained or to see revenged, but whatever information you are willing or able to communicate must be deferred."

"Nay," interrupted Ormond, with augmented vehemence, "art thou equally devoid of curiosity and justice? Thinkest thou that the enmity which bereft thy father of life will not seek thy own? There are evils which I cannot prevent thee from enduring, but there are, likewise, ills which my counsel will enable thee and thy friend to shun. Save me from witnessing thy death. Thy father's destiny is sealed; all that remained was to punish his assassin; but thou and thy Sophia still live. Why should ye perish by a like stroke?"

This intimation was sufficient to arrest the steps of Constantia. She withdrew her hand from the door, and fixed eyes of the deepest anxiety on Ormond: —"What mean you? How am I to understand—"

"Ah!" said Ormond, "I see thou wilt consent to stay. Thy detention shall not be long. Remain where thou art during one moment,—merely while I drag hither thy enemy and show thee a visage which thou wilt not be slow to recognise." Saying this, he hastily ascended the staircase, and quickly passed beyond her sight.

Deportment thus mysterious could not fail of bewildering her thoughts. There was somewhat in the looks and accents of Ormond, different from former appearances; tokens of a hidden purpose and a smothered meaning were perceptible,—a mixture of the inoffensive and the lawless, which, added to the loneliness and silence that encompassed her, produced a faltering emotion. Her curiosity was overpowered by her fear, and the resolution was suddenly conceived of seizing this opportunity to escape.

A third time she put her hand to the lock and attempted to open. The effort was ineffectual. The door that was accustomed to obey the gentlest touch was now immovable. She had lately unlocked and passed through it. Her eager inspection convinced her that the principal bolt was still withdrawn, but a small one was now perceived, of whose existence she had not been apprized, and over which her key had no power.

Now did she first harbour a fear that was intelligible in its dictates. Now did she first perceive herself sinking in the toils of some lurking enemy. Hope whispered that this foe was not Ormond. His conduct had bespoken no willingness to put constraint upon her steps. He talked not as if he was aware of this obstruction, and yet his seeming acquiescence might have flowed from a knowledge that she had no power to remove beyond his reach.

He warned her of danger to her life, of which he was her self-appointed rescuer. His counsel was to arm her with sufficient caution; the peril that awaited her was imminent; this was the time and place of its occurrence, and here she was compelled to remain, till the power that fastened would condescend to loose the door. There were other avenues to the hall. These were accustomed to be locked; but Ormond had found access, and, if all continued fast, it was incontestable that he was the author of this new impediment.

The other avenues were hastily examined. All were bolted and locked. The first impulse led her to call for help from without; but the mansion was distant from Laffert's habitation. This spot was wholly unfrequented. No passenger was likely to be stationed where her call could be heard. Besides, this forcible detention might operate for a short time, and be attended with no mischievous consequences. Whatever was to come, it was her duty to collect her courage and encounter it.

Tho steps of Ormond above now gave tokens of his approach. Vigilant observance of this man was all that her situation permitted. A vehement effort restored her to some degree of composure. Her stifled palpitations allowed her steadfastly to notice him as he now descended the stairs, bearing a lifeless body in his arms. "There!" said he, as he cast it at her feet; "whose countenance is that? Who would imagine that features like those belonged to an assassin and impostor?"

Closed eyelids and fallen muscles could not hide from her lineaments so often seen. She shrunk back and exclaimed, "Thomas Craig!"

A pause succeeded, in which she alternately gazed at the countenance of this unfortunate wretch and at Ormond. At length, the latter exclaimed,—

"Well, my girl, hast thou examined him? Dost thou recognise a friend or an enemy?"

"I know him well: but how came this? What purpose brought him hither? Who was the author of his fate?"

"Have I not already told thee that Ormond was his own avenger and thine? To thee and to me he has been a robber. To him thy father is indebted for the loss not only of property but life. Did crimes like these merit a less punishment? And what recompense is due to him whose vigilance pursued him hither and made him pay for his offences with his blood? What benefit have I received at thy hand to authorize me, for thy sake, to take away his life?"

"No benefit received from me," said Constantia, "would justify such an act. I should have abhorred myself for annexing to my benefits so bloody a condition. It calls for no gratitude or recompense. Its suitable attendant is remorse. That he is a thief, I know but too well; that my father died by his hand is incredible. No motives or means—"

"Why so?" interrupted Ormond. "Does not sleep seal up the senses? Cannot closets be unlocked at midnight? Cannot adjoining houses communicate by doors? Cannot these doors be hidden from suspicion by a sheet of canvas?"

These words were of startling and abundant import. They reminded her of circumstances in her father's chamber, which sufficiently explained the means by which his life was assailed. The closet, and its canvas-covered wall; the adjoining house untenanted and shut up—but this house, though unoccupied, belonged to Ormond. From the inferences which flowed hence, her attention was withdrawn by her companion, who continued:—

"Do these means imply the interposal of a miracle? His motives? What scruples can be expected from a man inured from infancy to cunning and pillage? Will he abstain from murder when urged by excruciating poverty, by menaces of persecution, by terror of expiring on the gallows?"

Tumultuous suspicions were now awakened in the mind of Constantia. Her faltering voice scarcely allowed her to ask, "How know *you* that Craig was thus guilty?—that these were his incitements and means?"

Ormond's solemnity now gave place to a tone of sarcasm and looks of exultation:—"Poor Constantia! Thou art still pestered with incredulity and doubts! My veracity is still in question! My knowledge, girl, is infallible. That these were his means of access I cannot be ignorant, for I pointed them out. He was urged by these motives, for they were stated and enforced by me. His was the deed, for I stood beside him when it was done."

These, indeed, were terms that stood in no need of further explanation. The veil that shrouded this formidable being was lifted high enough to make him be regarded with inexplicable horror. What his future acts should be, how his omens of ill were to be solved, were still involved in uncertainty.

In the midst of fears for her own safety, by which Constantia was now assailed, the image of her father was revived; keen regret and vehement upbraiding were conjured up.

"Craig, then, was the instrument, and yours the instigation, that destroyed my father! In what had he offended you? What cause had he given for resentment?"

"Cause!" replied he, with impetuous accents. "Resentment! None. My motive was benevolent; my deed conferred a benefit. I gave him sight and took away his life, from motives equally wise. Know you not that Ormond was fool enough to set value on the affections of a woman? These were sought with preposterous anxiety and endless labour. Among other facilitators of his purpose, he summoned gratitude to his aid. To snatch you from poverty, to restore his sight to your father, were expected to operate as incentives to love.

"But here I was the dupe of error. A thousand prejudices stood in my way. These, provided our intercourse were not obstructed, I hoped to subdue. The rage of innovation seized your father: this, blended with a mortal antipathy to me, made him labour to seduce you from the bosom of your peaceful country; to make you enter on a boisterous sea; to visit lands where all is havoc and hostility; to snatch you from the influence of my arguments.

"This new obstacle I was bound to remove. While revolving the means, chance and his evil destiny threw Craig in my way. I soon convinced him that his reputation and his life were in my hands. His retention of these depended upon my will, on the performance of conditions which I prescribed.

"My happiness and yours depended on your concurrence with my wishes. Your father's life was an obstacle to your concurrence. For killing him, therefore, I may claim your gratitude. His death was a due and disinterested offering at the altar of your felicity and mine.

"My deed was not injurious to him. At his age, death, whose coming at some period is inevitable, could not be distant. To make it unforeseen and brief, and void of pain,—to preclude the torments of a lingering malady, a slow and visible descent to the grave,—was the dictate of beneficence. But of what value was a continuance of his life? Either you would have gone with him to Europe or have stayed at home with me. In the first case, his life would have been rapidly consumed by perils and cares. In the second, separation from you, and union with me,—a being so detestable,—would equally have poisoned his existence.

"Craig's cowardice and crimes made him a pliant and commodious tool. I pointed out the way. The unsuspected door which led into the closet of your father's chamber was made, by my direction, during the life of Helena. By this avenue I was wont to post myself where all your conversations could be overheard. By this avenue an entrance and retreat were afforded to the agent of my newest purpose.

"Fool that I was! I solaced myself with the belief that all impediments were now smoothed, when a new enemy appeared. My folly lasted as long as my hope. I saw that to gain your affections, fortified by antiquated scruples and obsequious to the guidance of this new monitor, was impossible. It is not my way to toil after that which is beyond my reach. If the greater good be inaccessible, I learn to be contented with the less.

"I have served you with successless sedulity. I have set an engine in act to obliterate an obstacle to your felicity, and lay your father at rest. Under my guidance, this engine was productive only of good. Governed by itself or by another, it will only work you harm. I have, therefore, hastened to destroy it. Lo! it is now before you motionless and impotent.

"For this complexity of benefit I look for no reward. I am not tired of well-doing. Having ceased to labour for an unattainable good, I have come hither to possess myself of all that I now crave, and by the same deed to afford you an illustrious opportunity to signalize your wisdom and your fortitude."

During this speech, the mind of Constantia became more deeply pervaded with dread of some overhanging but incomprehensible evil. The strongest impulse was to gain a safe asylum, at a distance from this spot and from the presence of this extraordinary being. This impulse was followed by the recollection that her liberty was taken away, that egress from the hall was denied her, and that this restriction might be part of some conspiracy of Ormond against her life.

Security from danger like this would be, in the first place, sought, by one of Constantia's sex and opinions, in flight. This had been rendered, by some fatal chance or by the precautions of her foe, impracticable. Stratagem or force was all that remained to elude or disarm her adversary. For the contrivance and execution of fraud, all the habits of her life and all the maxims of her education had conspired to unfit her. Her force of muscles would avail her nothing against the superior energy of Ormond.

She remembered that to inflict death was no iniquitous exertion of self-defence, and that the penknife which she held in her hand was capable of this service. She had used it to remove any lurking obstruction in the wards of her key, supposing, for a time, this to be the cause of her failing to withdraw the bolt of the door. This resource was, indeed, scarcely less disastrous and deplorable than any fate from which it could rescue her. Some uncertainty still involved the intentions of Ormond. As soon as he paused, she spoke:—

"How am I to understand this prelude? Let me know the full extent of my danger,—why it is that I am hindered from leaving this house, and why this interview was sought."

"Ah, Constantia, this, indeed, is merely a prelude to a scene that is to terminate my influence over thy fate. When this is past I have sworn to part with thee forever. Art thou still dubious of my purpose? Art thou not a woman? And have I not entreated for thy love and been rejected?

"Canst thou imagine that I aim at thy life? My avowals of love were sincere; my passion was vehement and undisguised. It gave dignity and value to a gift in thy power, as a woman, to bestow. This has been denied. That gift has lost none of its value in my eyes. What thou refusest to bestow it is in my power to extort. I came for that end. When this end is accomplished, I will restore thee to liberty."

These words were accompanied by looks that rendered all explanation of their meaning useless. The evil reserved for her, hitherto obscured by half-disclosed and contradictory attributes, was now sufficiently apparent. The truth in this respect unveiled itself with the rapidity and brightness of an electrical flash.

She was silent. She cast her eyes at the windows and doors. Escape through them was hopeless. She looked at those lineaments of Ormond which evinced his disdain of supplication and inexorable passions. She felt that entreaty and argument would be vain; that all appeals to his compassion and benevolence would counteract her purpose, since, in the unexampled conformation of this man's mind, these principles were made subservient to his most flagitious designs. Considerations of justice and pity were made, by a fatal perverseness of reasoning, champions and bulwarks of his most atrocious mistakes.

The last extremes of opposition, the most violent expedients for defence, would be justified by being indispensable. To find safety for her honour, even in the blood of an assailant, was the prescription of duty. Tho equity of this species of defence was not, in the present confusion of her mind, a subject of momentary doubt.

To forewarn him of her desperate purpose would be to furnish him with means of counteraction. Her weapon would easily be wrested from her feeble hand. Ineffectual opposition would only precipitate her evil destiny. A rage, contented with nothing less than her life, might be awakened in his bosom. But was not this to be desired? Death, untimely and violent, was better than the loss of honour.

This thought led to a new series of reflections. She involuntarily shrunk from the act of killing: but would her efforts to destroy her adversary be effectual? Would not his strength and dexterity easily repel or elude them? Her power in this respect was questionable, but her power was undeniably sufficient to a different end. The instrument which could not rescue her from this injury by the destruction of another might save her from it by her own destruction.

These thoughts rapidly occurred; but the resolution to which they led was scarcely formed, when Ormond advanced towards her. She recoiled a few steps, and, showing the knife which she held, said,—

"Ormond! Beware! Know that my unalterable resolution is to die uninjured. I have the means in my power. Stop where you are; one step more, and I plunge this knife into my heart. I know that to contend with your strength or your reason would be vain. To turn this weapon against you I should not fear, if I were sure of success; but to that I will not trust. To save a greater good by the sacrifice of life is in my power, and that sacrifice shall be made."

"Poor Constantia!" replied Ormond, in a tone of contempt; "so thou preferrest thy imaginary honour to life! To escape this injury without a name or substance, without connection with the past or future, without contamination of thy purity or thraldom of thy will, thou wilt kill thyself; put an end to thy activity in virtue's cause; rob thy friend of her solace, the world of thy beneficence, thyself of being and pleasure?

"I shall be grieved for the fatal issue of my experiment; I shall mourn over thy martyrdom to the most opprobrious and contemptible of all errors: but that thou shouldst undergo the trial is decreed. There is still an interval of hope that thy cowardice is counterfeited, or that it will give place to wisdom and courage.

"Whatever thou intendest by way of prevention or cure, it behooves thee to employ with steadfastness. Die with the guilt of suicide and the brand of cowardice upon thy memory, or live with thy claims to felicity and approbation undiminished. Choose which thou wilt. Thy decision is of moment to thyself, but of none to me. Living or dead, the prize that I have in view shall be mine."

CHAPTER X.

It will be requisite to withdraw your attention from this scene for a moment, and fix it on myself. My impatience of my friend's delay, for some days preceding this disastrous interview, became continually more painful. As the time of our departure approached, my dread of some misfortune or impediment increased. Ormond's disappearance from the scene contributed but little to my consolation. To wrap his purposes in mystery, to place himself at seeming distance, was the usual artifice of such as he,—was necessary to the maturing of his project and the hopeless entanglement of his victim. I saw no means of placing the safety of my friend beyond his reach. Between different methods of procedure, there was, however, room for choice. Her present abode was more hazardous than an abode in the city. To be alone argued a state more defenceless and perilous than to be attended by me.

I wrote her an urgent admonition to return. My remonstrances were couched in such terms as, in my own opinion, laid her under the necessity of immediate compliance. The letter was despatched by the usual messenger, and for some hours I solaced myself with the prospect of a speedy meeting.

These thoughts gave place to doubt and apprehension. I began to distrust the efficacy of my arguments, and to invent a thousand reasons, inducing her, in defiance of my rhetoric, at least to protract her absence. These reasons I had not previously conceived, and had not, therefore, attempted, in my letter, to invalidate their force. This omission was possible to be supplied in a second epistle; but, meanwhile, time would be lost, and my new arguments might, like the old, fail to convince her. At least, the tongue was a much more versatile and powerful advocate than the pen; and, by hastening to her habitation, I might either compel her to return with me, or ward off danger by

67

my presence, or share it with her. I finally resolved to join her by the speediest conveyance.

This resolution was suggested by the meditations of a sleepless night. I rose with the dawn, and sought out the means of transporting myself, with most celerity, to the abode of my friend. A stage-boat, accustomed twice a day to cross New York Bay to Staten Island, was prevailed upon, by liberal offers, to set out upon the voyage at the dawn of day. The sky was gloomy, and the air boisterous and unsettled. The wind, suddenly becoming tempestuous and adverse, rendered the voyage at once tedious and full of peril. A voyage of nine miles was not effected in less than eight hours and without imminent and hairbreadth danger of being drowned.

Fifteen miles of the journey remained to be performed by land. A carriage, with the utmost difficulty, was procured, but lank horses and a crazy vehicle were but little in unison with my impatience. We reached not Amboy ferry till some hours after nightfall. I was rowed across the Sound, and proceeded to accomplish the remainder of my journey—about three miles—on foot.

I was actuated to this speed by indefinite but powerful motives. The belief that my speedy arrival was essential to the rescue of my friend from some inexplicable injury haunted me with ceaseless importunity. On no account would I have consented to postpone this precipitate expedition till the morrow.

I at length arrived at Dudley's farm-house. The inhabitants were struck with wonder at the sight of me. My clothes were stained by the water by which every passenger was copiously sprinkled during our boisterous navigation, and soiled by dust; my frame was almost overpowered by fatigue and abstinence.

To my anxious inquiries respecting my friend, they told me that her evenings were usually spent at the mansion, where it was probable she was now to be found. They were not apprized of any inconvenience or danger that betided her. It was her custom sometimes to prolong her absence till midnight.

I could not applaud the discretion nor censure the temerity of this proceeding. My mind was harassed by unintelligible omens and self-confuted fears. To obviate the danger and to banish my inquietudes was my first duty. For this end I hastened to the mansion. Having passed the intervening hillocks and copses, I gained a view of the front of the building. My heart suddenly sunk, on observing that no apartment—not even that in which I knew it was her custom to sit at these unseasonable hours—was illuminated. A gleam from the window of the study I should have regarded as an argument at once of her presence and her safety.

I approached the house with misgiving and faltering steps. The gate leading into a spacious court was open. A sound on one side attracted my attention. In the present state of my thoughts, any near or unexplained sound sufficed to startle me. Looking towards the quarter whence my panic was excited, I espied, through the dusk, a horse grazing, with his bridle thrown over his neck.

This appearance was a new source of perplexity and alarm. The inference was unavoidable that a visitant was here. Who that visitant was, and how he was now employed, was a subject of eager but fruitless curiosity. Within and around the mansion, all was buried in the deepest repose. I now approached the principal door, and, looking through the keyhole, perceived a lamp, standing on the lowest step of the staircase. It shed a pale light over the lofty ceiling and marble balustrades. No face or movement of a human being was perceptible.

These tokens assured me that some one was within: they also accounted for the non-appearance of light at the window above. I withdrew my eye from this avenue, and was preparing to knock loudly for admission, when my attention was awakened by some one who advanced to the door from the inside and seemed busily engaged in unlocking. I started back and waited with impatience till the door should open and the person issue forth.

Presently I heard a voice within exclaim, in accents of mingled terror and grief, "Oh, what—what will become of me? Shall I never be released from this detested prison?"

The voice was that of Constantia. It penetrated to my heart like an icebolt. I once more darted a glance through the crevice. A figure, with difficulty recognised to be that of my friend, now appeared in sight. Her hands were clasped on her breast, her eyes wildly fixed upon the ceiling and streaming with tears, and her hair unbound and falling confusedly over her bosom and neck.

My sensations scarcely permitted me to call, "Constantia! For Heaven's sake, what has happened to you? Open the door, I beseech you."

"What voice is that? Sophia Courtland! O my friend! I am imprisoned! Some demon has barred the door, beyond my power to unfasten. Ah, why comest thou so late? Thy succour would have somewhat profited if sooner given; but now, the lost Constantia—" Here her voice sunk into convulsive sobs.

In the midst of my own despair, on perceiving the fulfilment of my apprehensions, and what I regarded as the fatal execution of some project of Ormond, I was not insensible to the suggestions of prudence. I entreated my friend to retain her courage, while I flew to Laffert's and returned with suitable assistance to burst open the door.

The people of the farm-house readily obeyed my summons. Accompanied by three men of powerful sinews, sons and servants of the farmer, I returned with the utmost expedition to the mansion. The lamp still remained in its former place, but our loudest calls were unanswered. The silence was uninterrupted and profound.

The door yielded to strenuous and repeated efforts, and I rushed into the hall. The first object that met my sight was my friend, stretched upon the floor, pale and motionless, supine, and with all the tokens of death.

From this object my attention was speedily attracted by two figures, breathless and supine like that of Constantia. One of them was Ormond. A smile of disdain still sat upon his features. The wound by which he fell was secret, and was scarcely betrayed by the effusion of a drop of blood. The face of the third victim was familiar to my early days. It was that of the impostor whose artifice had torn from Mr. Dudley his peace and fortune.

An explication of this scene was hopeless. By what disastrous and inscrutable fate a place like this became the scene of such complicated havoc, to whom Craig was indebted for his death, what evil had been meditated or inflicted by Ormond, and by what means his project had arrived at this bloody consummation, were topics of wild and fearful conjecture.

But my friend—the first impulse of my fears was to regard her as dead. Hope and a closer observation outrooted, or, at least, suspended, this opinion. One of the men lifted her in his arms. No trace of blood or mark of fatal violence was discoverable, and the effusion of cold water restored her, though slowly, to life.

To withdraw her from this spectacle of death was my first care. She suffered herself to be led to the farm-house. She was carried to her chamber. For a time she appeared incapable of recollection. She grasped my hand, as I sat by her bedside, but scarcely gave any other tokens of life.

From this state of inactivity she gradually recovered. I was actuated by a thousand forebodings, but refrained from molesting her by interrogation or condolence. I watched by her side in silence, but was eager to collect from her own lips an account of this mysterious transaction.

At length she opened her eyes, and appeared to recollect her present situation, and the events which led to it. I inquired into her condition, and asked if there were any thing in my power to procure or perform for her.

"Oh, my friend," she answered, "what have I done, what have I suffered, within the last dreadful hour! The remembrance, though insupportable, will never leave me. You can do nothing for my relief. All I claim is your compassion and your sympathy."

"I hope," said I, "that nothing has happened to load you with guilt or with shame?"

"Alas! I know not. My deed was scarcely the fruit of intention. It was suggested by a momentary frenzy. I saw no other means of escaping from vileness and pollution. I was menaced with an evil worse than death. I forebore till my strength was almost subdued: the lapse of another moment would have placed me beyond hope.

"My stroke was desperate and at random. It answered my purpose too well. He cast at me a look of terrible upbraiding, but spoke not. His heart was pierced, and he sunk, as if struck by lightning, at my feet. O much erring and unhappy Ormond! That thou shouldst thus untimely perish! That I should be thy executioner!"

These words sufficiently explained the scene that I had witnessed. The violence of Ormond had been repulsed by equal violence. His foul attempts had been prevented by his death. Not to deplore the necessity which had produced this act was impossible; but, since this necessity existed, it was surely not a deed to be thought upon with lasting horror, or to be allowed to generate remorse.

In consequence of this catastrophe, arduous duties had devolved upon me. The people that surrounded me were powerless with terror. Their ignorance and cowardice left them at a loss how to act in this emergency. They besought my direction, and willingly performed whatever I thought proper to enjoin upon them.

No deliberation was necessary to acquaint me with my duty. Laffert was despatched to the nearest magistrate with a letter, in which his immediate presence was entreated and these transactions were briefly explained. Early the next day the formalities of justice, in the inspection of the bodies and the examination of witnesses, were executed. It would be needless to dwell on the particulars of this catastrophe. A sufficient explanation has been given of the causes that led to it. They were such as exempted my friend from legal animadversion. Her act was prompted by motives which every scheme of jurisprudence known in the world not only exculpates, but applauds. To state these motives before a tribunal hastily formed and exercising its functions on the spot was a task not to be avoided, though infinitely painful. Remonstrances the most urgent and pathetic could scarcely conquer her reluctance.

This task, however, was easy, in comparison with that which remained. To restore health and equanimity to my friend; to repel the erroneous accusations of her conscience; to hinder her from musing, with eternal anguish, upon this catastrophe; to lay the spirit of secret upbraiding by which she was incessantly tormented, which bereft her of repose, empoisoned all her enjoyments, and menaced not only the subversion of her peace but the speedy destruction of her life, became my next employment.

My counsels and remonstrances were not wholly inefficacious. They afforded me the prospect of her ultimate restoration to tranquillity. Meanwhile, I called to my aid the influence of time and of a change of scene. I hastened to embark with her for Europe. Our voyage was tempestuous and dangerous, but storms and perils at length gave way to security and repose.

Before our voyage was commenced, I endeavoured to procure tidings of the true condition and designs of Ormond. My information extended no further than that he had put his American property into the hands of Mr. Melbourne, and was preparing to embark for France. Courtland, who has since been at Paris, and who, while there, became confidentially acquainted with Martinette de Beauvais, has communicated facts of an unexpected nature.

At the period of Ormond's return to Philadelphia, at which his last interview with Constantia in that city took place, he visited Martinette. He avowed himself to be her brother, and supported his pretensions by relating the incidents of his early life. A separation at the age of fifteen, and which had lasted for the same number of years, may be supposed to have considerably changed the countenance and figure she had formerly known. His relationship was chiefly proved by the enumeration of incidents of which her brother only could be apprized.

He possessed a minute acquaintance with her own adventures, but concealed from her the means by which he had procured the knowledge. He had rarely and imperfectly alluded to his own opinions and projects, and had maintained an invariable silence on the subject of his connection with Constantia and Helena. Being informed of her intention to return to France, he readily complied with her request to accompany her in this voyage. His intentions in this respect were frustrated by the dreadful catastrophe that has been just related. Respecting this event, Martinette had collected only vague and perplexing information. Courtland, though able to remove her doubts, thought proper to withhold from her the knowledge he possessed.

Since her arrival in England, the life of my friend has experienced little variation. Of her personal deportment and domestic habits you have been a witness. These, therefore, it would be needless for me to exhibit. It is sufficient to have related events which the recentness of your intercourse with her hindered you from knowing but by means of some formal narrative like the present. She and her friend only were able to impart to you the knowledge which you have so anxiously sought. In consideration of your merits and of your attachment to my friend, I have consented to devote my leisure to this task.

It is now finished; and I have only to add my wishes that the perusal of this tale may afford you as much instruction as the contemplation of the sufferings and vicissitudes of Constantia Dudley has afforded to me. Farewell.

THE END.

Ingram Content Group UK Ltd.
Milton Keynes UK
UKHW040637190323
418778UK00003B/34

9 783752 382594